Nightmare of Dream Creek

An Alaskan Bear Tale

Nightmare of Dream Creek

An Alaskan Bear Tale

Ted Gerken

Northwest Publishing, Inc.
Salt Lake City, Utah

Nightmare of Dream Creek—An Alaskan Bear Tale

All rights reserved.
Copyright © 1996 Northwest Publishing, Inc.

Reproduction in any manner, in whole or in part,
in English or in other languages, or otherwise
without written permission of the publisher is prohibited.

This is a work of fiction.
All characters and events portrayed in this book are fictional,
and any resemblance to real people or incidents is purely coincidental.

For information address: Northwest Publishing, Inc.
6906 South 300 West, Salt Lake City, Utah 84047
CR/JB 10-16-95

PRINTING HISTORY
First Printing 1996

ISBN: 1-56901-677-1

NPI books are published by Northwest Publishing, Incorporated,
6906 South 300 West, Salt Lake City, Utah 84047.
The name "NPI" and the "NPI" logo are trademarks belonging to
Northwest Publishing, Incorporated.

PRINTED IN THE UNITED STATES OF AMERICA.
10 9 8 7 6 5 4 3 2 1

Preface

Although Walleye is a fictional bear, his story is true. I've spent hundreds of days and thousands of hours observing the behavior of coastal grizzlies in their natural habitat on Kodiak Island, the Alaska Peninsula, and the Kamishak Bay and Iliamna watersheds. For 20 years I've watched this situation develop in the bush; the bizarre behavior, the confrontational attitudes, the instinctive responses of both humans and grizzlies as each pursues its chosen course of life. Most of the incidents involving Walleye and the other bears in the story were personally observed by the author. To fill in places where my own personal knowledge was inadequate, I have added some of the first-hand incidents told to me by reliable friends and clients.

Dream Creek, Gibraltar Lake, Iliamna, Kakhonak, the McNeil River and Kamishak Bay are real. The enormous salmon runs of both drainages occur every year. The coastal grizzlies feed and flourish on the bonanza of protein from the salmon every season. The bears live and die according to their nature—when man interferes he compounds their problems. And his own!

Acknowledgments

I should like to acknowledge certain contributions to the story. First, to my wife Mary for her patience, encouragement, and understanding as I spent so many weeks and months at the manuscript.

To Angus Cameron of Wilton, Connecticut, who encouraged me to start writing and supported my feeble beginnings with both praise and criticism, as needed, to keep my mind on the correct track;

To my sister Anne Silleck who spent so much time editing the manuscript, and the following individuals who contributed tales of their own:

Lt. Malcolm Smith, U.S. Coast Guard helicopter pilot stationed with me at the Coast Guard Base and Air Station, Kodiak, Alaska;

Joe Abrams, Alaska State Trooper assigned as Fish and Wildlife Protection Officer in Iliamna, Alaska;
Ken Wynne, DDS. of Anchorage, Alaska;
Bill Ryer of Claremont, New Hampshire;
Gene Ruth of Providence, Rhode Island;
Bob Glen of Anchorage, Alaska;
Scott Lawrence of King Salmon, Alaska;
Bill Holden of Anchorage, Alaska.

1

    I want to tell you a story about two men and a bear. It's not a very nice story, but then Walleye wasn't a very nice bear. He was nice enough at the beginning—docile and shy, the kind of bear who stayed out of harm's way, who'd shamble away from humans whenever he could—and he stayed that way as long as the few humans he came across treated him with equal respect. But that was before he met Cal, and after a few encounters with that character, Walleye turned into an 800-pound coastal grizzly with a grudge—a crafty and devious carnivore who'd lost his natural fear of humans and stalked the salmon streams of Alaska with a vengeance.
    It all started when my nephew, hunting guide Bill

Bascomb of Kodiak, contracted to take Cal bear hunting in Alaska.

Most of Bill's hunters were sportsmen, men and women as equally interested in their surroundings and the excitement of the chase as they were in taking a bear rug home. Then Cal arrived.

Bill picked up Cal Edgecombe at the Kodiak airport and flew him to the hunting camp along the southwestern shore of Kamishak Bay. Although it was mid-April, snow still covered the open hills above a thousand feet; below that, patches of ice and snow still lay in the gullies and ravines where winter storms had heaped the drifts as tall as a moose's back. The large spruce forests on the other side of the bay gave way to scrubby alder and willow patches around Bill's hunting camp, a 16' x 24' four-man cabin built not far from the western end of a long, narrow, cobble gravel bar Bill used as a runway.

The only visible sign of spring was the open water in the tiny stream that rippled past the cabin and the ten square feet of open water where the creek flowed into the lake; everything else was still frozen, including the ground that crunched under their feet with every step. Down near the creek, where the boggy ground held water, myriad spines of ice now jutted their frosty tips through the mossy leaves. Along the rest of the trails Bill had cut around the cabin, the ground was as hard as granite.

After breakfast, Bill, accompanied by his assistant guide, John Doverman, took Cal on a hike up into the hills to one of Bill's favorite lookout points. It was the open end of a wide valley. A small stream meandered down the valley floor while acres of gray-barked, 15-foot-tall alders alternated with fields of dead grass to form a patchwork quilt of tan, brown, gray, and white snow patches on the surrounding hills. They set up a spotting scope and settled down to watch and wait, John scanning the hills with the scope while Bill used binoculars. And there they stayed all morning, eating a cold lunch of sandwiches washed down with lukewarm coffee from a thermos.

"Can't see why we have to sit here all day," Cal grumbled, halfway through the afternoon. He opened another can of beer, flipped the tab on the ground, and tossed the empty he'd just finished into the alders.

Bill had already asked him twice before not to litter the place. He didn't much like the filtered cigarette butts Cal had scattered around either, and he'd tried to ignore them, but beer cans were another matter. Before Bill could say anything, John jumped down and retrieved the can.

John was Bill's nephew, his only sister's kid, a tough stringy guy of 28 who wanted to be a bear guide. Bill had taken him on as an apprentice three years ago and never regretted it. John could pack his own weight—some of the fresh bear hides they'd taken weighed well over a hundred pounds—and carry it a mile across the tundra without stopping, then cut and split a cord of firewood before dinner. Unlike many other Alaskans who sported full beards, John was clean-shaven, with a mop of dark brown hair he kept tied in a knot behind his head. He wasn't much of a talker, but he loved Alaska and was even more of a nut than Bill about keeping it the way it is, wild and free and clean.

"You can see there aren't any bears in this valley," Cal said, barely noticing John's efforts. "Why don't we climb over the ridge and look at the next one?"

"If we spread our scent all over the valley, there won't be any bears anywhere," Bill told him—for the third time. Cal had been in camp only one day and already he was getting on Bill's nerves.

"Hey, boss," John called softly; he always insisted on calling Bill boss whenever they had outsiders in camp. "I think we've got one."

John had good eyes, almost as good as Bill's, but then he'd been in training for three years. Quickly scanning the slope across the valley where John was looking, Bill picked out the bear slowly walking around the side of a large, tree-covered knoll. It was crossing a wide field of dead grass and its light brown hide stood out clearly against the blond grass.

"Where?" Cal wanted to know. He couldn't find it in his own $700 binoculars, so Bill moved over to stand in front of him and point out the bear.

"Look along my arm," Bill said. "See the knoll? All the way across the valley and just underneath the ridge line? The bear's in the field just below it."

"It keeps looking back over its shoulder, boss," John said, tracking the bear in his scope, "almost like it's being followed."

John was right; the bear kept turning its head as if there were something back there it wanted to keep track of. Then Bill spotted the second bear and pointed it out to Cal. It was so much larger that Cal, now a one-day expert, immediately yelled, "It's a sow with a cub!"

"Sows don't follow cubs," Bill said. "They lead."

The first bear was a sow in heat, and the second a boar. Nothing else would bring two grizzlies together in the spring, and Bill knew it—but this was the biggest boar he'd seen in five years.

"Remember that great big boar I told you about, John?" Bill whispered.

"The Warden?"

"Yeah—that dark chocolate-colored monster I met up with a few years ago. I think we're looking at him."

"He must be almost 20 years old now," John said.

Bill nodded—at least 20, maybe 22, and they don't live much past 25 in the wild. It's hard to tell just how old the really big ones are until you get a tooth to examine—and that isn't easy. Three times Bill had tried for him with other clients, but every time the bear had outsmarted him and escaped without a shot being fired. But those times he hadn't had a sow with him as a distraction. "Just my luck," Bill thought. "This could be my best chance at that monster. Why'd I have to spot such a trophy with a clown like Cal along?"

Seeing an animal like that is one thing; getting close enough for a shot is something else again. Bill knew the first thing they had to do was try and figure out what the bears were going to do next—and the only way to do that was to sit right where they were and watch them for a while. John adjusted the lens on the spotting scope and steadied each of its three legs, pushing them into the partially frozen ground. When he stepped back, Bill and Cal each took a better look with the higher magnification of the scope. Although the temperature was less than 50 degrees, heat waves from the valley floor blurred their vision. The bears were over a mile away.

"So what are we going to do, sit here all day?" Cal asked. "Let's go get him!"

Bill expected that. "There's a lot more to bear hunting than just shooting everything that turns up," he said. "Let's see what condition the hide's in first." If a boar's been out of hibernation for a while, he may have been rubbing and scratching against trees and rocks; if so, the hide would be almost worthless by now, with most of the long guard hairs broken off.

"So what about the sow?" Cal asked.

"She's legal," Bill said—which she was, not having any cubs with her. "And she probably hasn't been out of hibernation as long as the boar, so she stands a better chance of having a hide in good condition. But I thought you wanted a real trophy."

"I want a bear, plain enough?"

Although the female was a good-sized sow, as sows go, she was nowhere near the size of the boar. If it was The Warden, Bill knew he'd square over ten feet. Even if it wasn't The Warden, the boar in sight probably weighed close to a thousand pounds. The sow was considerably smaller; if they squared her hide, she'd probably stretch over seven feet. She looked a good 600 pounds but, again, from that distance it was all guesstimate. They had to get closer.

The two bears stopped to feed on roots in a small alder patch. The hunters could see their shapes as they moved about under the leafless branches of the trees, digging with their front feet at the roots lying just under the snow. After half an hour of this, the two bears moved out into the grassy open hillside and lay down only 20 feet from each other. They were a mating pair, that was obvious now, and if Bill and John and Cal waited and watched them for another six hours, they'd probably see them actually joined together. Bill and John had waited like this with other clients, but with Cal around they didn't have time to wait.

In the past Bill often let John take the client on the last phase of a hunt, to give him the experience. But this time Bill wasn't so sure John wouldn't just as soon shoot Cal as the bear, so Bill figured he'd better do it himself. Besides, if it was The Warden, Bill wanted to be there.

John and Bill figured out the route they'd have to take across the valley to get upwind of the bear. John would have to keep an eye both on the bears and on Cal and Bill because, if the bears moved, Cal and Bill wouldn't be able to see them from where they'd be. They'd already worked out a system of hand signals for these situations: if John held both arms straight up it meant the bears were behind Bill; both arms straight down meant the bears were ahead of him; right or left arm extended meant the bears were that way and not moving; right or left arm waving meant the bears were moving in that direction.

Before they left for the stalk, Bill wanted to be sure John understood the procedure they'd used to communicate. "We'll be over a mile away, so keep an eye on both us and the bears. When you see me looking back at you with my glasses, and I raise my arm, that's the time to signal."

"What if they split up?" John asked.

"I don't think they'll separate but, if they do, concentrate on the big one," Bill said and turned to Cal. "Are you ready?"

"I've been ready for four years," the hunter said and picked up his rifle, a custom-made, finely engraved, bolt-action .300 Winchester magnum. "Let's do it."

Cal Edgecombe was 50 years old that year, a self-made millionaire and one-time two-letter man from Georgia Tech, football and baseball he'd bragged. He was about 5'9" but his waistline now exceeded his chest by several inches. A faint trace of blood vessels across his nose belied where he fought most of his battles these days—that and the half-dozen bottles of expensive bourbon and two cases of beer he'd brought into camp with him.

Cal was dressed in the finest hunting clothes that Abercrombie and Fitch of New York sold, and looked like a proper European gentleman: olive knickers and socks tucked into the top of fine-grained leather boots, a matching jacket of wool with a leather shooting pad on the right shoulder, and a soft-brimmed felt hat with a small red feather in the band. A pair of yellow shooting glasses hung from a lanyard around his neck.

If Cal had spent more time on his physical conditioning, the hunt would have gone better for him. Bill had to keep stopping to wait for Cal to catch up, puffing and red-faced, and the stalk took longer than it should have. The uneven ground under the dried grass was difficult to walk on and, when they crossed through several alder patches, they had to walk through a foot of soft snow. Once across the creek, they climbed a series of knolls that put them well above Bill's last sighting of the bears. An hour later, when Bill focused his glasses on the lookout, John was looking back at him through the scope.

Bill raised an arm over his head and John immediately

dropped both arms to his side. "The bears haven't moved, Cal," Bill said softly. "They should be directly downhill about 300 yards away."

The hillside had looked almost flat from the lookout; now they could see it was full of knolls and depressions. Bill knew that if they did it right, the knolls could help during the stalk. He decided to walk directly over each knoll rather than around them—better to spot the bears from above, if possible. A gentle breeze blew uphill from the bears to the hunters.

After checking their rifles, they started slowly down the hill, placing their feet carefully on the brittle grass to make as little noise as possible. As they topped each knoll, Bill stopped and raised his head slowly to peer at the slope beyond. When all looked clear, he motioned Cal to join him, and they started forward again. The pace was agonizingly slow, but it was the only way to get close enough to the bears before they ran for cover.

After 20 minutes, they'd covered all but the last knoll. Checking his bearings with John, Bill saw him start jumping up and down with both arms waving wildly in the air.

"What the hell does that mean?" Bill whispered.

Cal looked at him and raised his eyebrows. His pupils were tiny black orbs. Putting his mouth next to Cal's ear, Bill breathed, "Get ready, Cal. This is it."

A thin film of perspiration lined Cal's brow and he started to tremble slightly. His breath was coming in short gasps, either from the climb or something else. "You all right?" Bill asked, very quietly. This was a hell of a time for him to lose his nerve.

He nodded. "Then let's go," Bill said.

A dozen steps and they came to the base of the last knoll, a grass-covered hummock only about six feet high. Below, on each side of the knoll, they could see the alder-lined creek as it curved its way along the floor of the valley; only the hillside on the other side of the knoll was still hidden.

Slowly raising his head, Bill peered over the crest of the knoll, looking carefully across the grassy slope. He studied every line, curve, and indentation in the hillside below for a full minute. No bears. "I guess they're gone," he said.

But this time he was wrong. The bears were lying in a shallow depression less than 50 feet away—so close they heard his whispered voice. Instantly on their feet and running at full speed, they split up, the sow quickly disappearing into a draw down to the left, the huge boar galloping along the hillside to the right. It was The Warden, Bill was sure of it, and his hide was a mess. The dark brown guard hairs had been rubbed off both hindquarters. Even his back had been rubbed in places, exposing the lighter underfur. As a trophy, his hide was worthless.

He was already more than a hundred yards away and sprinting along the hillside in full flight. Bill had never gotten this close to him before; now that he saw him close up, he was sure it was a record-class animal that would probably place in the top 25. But he was as good as gone—they'd be lucky to see him again in a month.

Cra-a-ck! Cal's high-powered rifle exploded only ten feet from Bill's right ear. The huge, dark-chocolate colored grizzly bear was still in full view, now almost 200 yards away, and sprinting across the grassy slope. He was traveling over 30 miles an hour. "He's too far away!" Bill shouted.

Blam! Cal didn't care—the damn fool had waited all year to shoot a bear but now couldn't wait one more day for a killing shot. No, not Cal, he had to shoot at the first bear they saw. *Blam! Blam!* The bear reached a brushy ravine leading toward the distant hills and disappeared into it.

Bill had met only a few other men like Cal in his 20 years as a bear guide, men who treated the outdoors as their own private shooting gallery and fired at almost anything that moved. These were the same kind of men who'd gotten so soft with easy living they even wanted their hunting made easy for them. But they caused problems for everyone else—now it was Bill's job to follow the tracks up into that brushy ravine to make sure the bear wasn't lying up there wounded. And waiting.

There isn't much in this world that gets as mad as a wounded grizzly bear—especially a bear that size—and Bill already knew the kind of protective cover they liked to hide in: thick dense brush where you can't see more than 50 feet and where every stump, hummock, and knoll looks like a bear. Bill had learned long ago that you just don't shoot at a running bear that far away. He'd told the dumb sonofabitch not to shoot!

Silence returned after the loud bark of the four rifle shots. The valley was bathed in sunshine; small shadows scurried across the grass as little white clouds drifted in from the northwest. A flock of snow buntings twittered along the creek seeking the first buds of spring while two moose grazed at the edge of an alder and willow patch on the opposite slope, oblivious to the cacophony of noise from the hunter's side of the valley. Moose are like that; what they can't see or smell doesn't bother them.

"What do we do now?" Cal asked.

"Look for a blood trail."

2

They started looking for the trail at the large patch of flattened grass where the two bears had been lying down. Two sets of tracks were visible in the grass, the boar's leading across the hill to the right and the sow's downhill to the left. "What do we do?" Cal asked.

"Follow the boar," Bill said, pointing to the faint trail of disturbed grass leading toward a gully. "If you hit it, we should see some blood on the grass."

"What if we do?"

"Let's hope we don't. You take the uphill side of the trail and I'll take this side. Go slowly and look at everything—the ground, blades of grass, dried leaves, everything." Shouldering his rifle, an old .375 H&H Magnum

Winchester Model 70 that he'd carried for 25 years, Bill started along the faintly marked trail of broken grass.

The grass had grown three feet tall last summer and was now dried and lying over, with some of the clustered sheaves still six to eight inches above the frozen ground. They couldn't shuffle along but had to lift each foot in their slow progress over the meadow, careful not to disturb any of the grass until they'd examined each stem.

When he started, Bill was looking for bent or broken grass stems to show where the bear had run; when they got close to where the bear had been when Cal first fired, he slowed down even more, now looking for both broken grass and drops of blood. If one of Cal's shots had hit the animal and passed clean through it, blood might have sprayed on the downhill side, so Bill had to search both in the trail and alongside it.

Cal shuffled along beside him, walking in the trail when he moved to the side, then back out of it as Bill shifted toward him. Cal spent more time looking around the hillside than he did looking for the bear's trail; maybe he thought the bear was going to jump out at him. They were halfway to the ravine before Bill saw the first drop of blood.

"You hit him, Cal," he said, pointing to the trace of red on a single dried stem of grass at his feet.

"I knew I couldn't miss," Cal crowed. "Not something that big."

Bill just shook his head. The big oaf didn't even realize how dangerous that made everything. He'd find out soon enough just how much spine Cal had.

Continuing along the trail, they walked almost to the edge of the ravine before Bill spotted another trace of red. The bear probably hadn't been hit too badly if it was losing so little blood, but no one could ever be sure. Five years ago Bill had tracked a bear over a mile on just a few drops of blood and finally found it lying dead, shot through one lung. The bullet hadn't gone all the way through the animal and most of the blood had stayed inside the bear's chest cavity.

"Now what?" Cal asked, looking into the brush.

Bill knew he had to go into that alder-choked ravine; what he didn't know was whether he wanted Cal along. He'd been in alders before looking for a wounded bear; it's like stepping into the bear's backyard. The ravine was a dark tangle of twisted alders, willows, and pushki weed—the best kind of cover for the bear.

A grizzly is one of the toughest animals to kill cleanly, especially on a running shot like Cal's, and it probably wasn't wounded very badly. And it was also a monster bear—old, experienced, and cunning. Stalking him in the alders, Bill figured the odds were 50-50—the bear had as much chance of getting them as they had of getting it, even with a powerful rifle like his .375 magnum. With John and his rifle along, the odds would have been maybe 60-40 Bill's way, but with Cal, they could go 40-60 the other way.

"I'm going after him," Bill said. "I've got no choice, but you do. You can wait here or walk back to the lookout the way we came."

"I'm coming, too," Cal said. "You're not leaving me alone out here."

Bill took another look at his big brave client. He was sweating heavily; small rivulets of water coursed down both cheeks soaking his collar, larger drops dripped off his red nose. When he took off his wool cap, water glistened on the bald crown of his head and ran down into the sandy-colored hair around each ear. "Suit yourself," Bill said. "Reload your gun, with one round in the chamber, but keep the safety on. You're walking behind me and I don't want any accidents."

Cal started to tell Bill how much experience he'd had with weapons, but Bill pushed past him into the ravine. It was no time to try to convince him how good his client was with a rifle—he'd already seen him shoot.

It looked like the bear had stopped running as soon as it reached the ravine. The tracks were faint and difficult to follow: a turned leaf here, a nail print there in the crusty ground. They didn't see anymore blood until they crossed a patch of snow, where Bill found a dozen more drops, probably because they stood out clearly against the grayish-white, drifted snow. They were single drops, deep red and not frothy, so it wasn't a lung shot. And the bear was heading uphill—a badly wounded animal would have headed downhill toward the creek to submerge its body in the icy water for relief from the pain.

Cal stuck to Bill's heels like a magnet to steel, never more than a few steps behind. He'd become strangely quiet since they entered the thick brush that surrounded them inside the ravine. The air was cooler there and what daylight filtered through the overhanging branches was much darker. The tracks in the snow headed straight uphill for a quarter mile, then turned in a large circle a hundred yards across before heading uphill again.

The bear had taken more time selecting his route now, purposefully entering thicker growths of alder and willow. The possibility that he might be looking for a good place to lie down and wait was paramount on Bill's mind, but he didn't dare turn around and tell Cal, not that it would have done any good, anyway. This was Bill's game now.

Slowing even more, they inched along. With each half-step Bill stopped and slowly looked from side to side, trying to spot anything out of the ordinary. Every small hummock began to look like a chocolate-colored grizzly lying in wait, every frozen cranberry left over from last summer a bear's eye, every whitened twig on the ground a claw.

Bill knew he was hiding there somewhere—waiting— and if he didn't see the bear before the bear saw them, his charge would reach them in a second or two. At that range, only a lucky shot would kill him, and then his momentum would carry him right into the two of them.

The ravine was wider now, fed by gullies on both sides where small brooks bubbled quietly toward the valley floor. The ground was uneven and the brush thicker; several small hummocks made progress even harder. At times Bill couldn't see more than 30 feet in any direction. Then he noticed the tracks had started to circle again. Instead of going directly over a hummock, they went around it, then veered to the right instead of continuing uphill. Bill stopped so suddenly Cal bumped into his back.

There wasn't a breath of wind in the ravine. Bill didn't think the bear could smell them more than a hundred feet away; the only way he could know where they were was by the noise they made—and that wasn't much. Between patches of snow, the ground was covered with wet decaying leaves that muffled the sound of their boots.

Suddenly all hell broke loose. Two moose that had been resting within the ravine leaped to their feet and charged away to Bill's left, crashing through the thick brush as they ran for their lives. Cal screamed, and Bill spun around, thinking the bear had got him. He saw Cal drop his rifle, turn, and run back along the trail they'd just come in on. Cal didn't stop running until he got to the open meadow.

Bill caught a flash of the cow and calf; the loud crashing on the other side told him the bear was running also—but which way? He'd already eased the safety off his Winchester; now all he could do was wait. The bear was either charging or retreating—in the thick brush he didn't know which.

Bill didn't relax until he heard the bear turn uphill. Apparently the moose had defeated his ambush. In the confusion and noise of crashing brush, with both the moose and Cal running away, the bear decided to retreat—this time—but Bill knew now he'd be hiding in wait for him further up the hill.

But he might not have to follow him much farther. The

bear had probably been lying down in the snow waiting for them, so Bill walked to where all the noise had come from. Sure enough, the signs were there: many paw prints, a depression where the bear had lain down, and several drops of blood. The Warden had been waiting there for quite a while, and Bill studied the blood to see where on his body it might have come from. It looked as if each drop was either near or in the track of the bear's right front foot. Bill found several drops all together where his front feet had rested.

It looked like the bear might have a sore foot for a while but wasn't too badly hurt. He'd survive—and be even smarter the next time.

Bill wasn't too sure about Cal. Retracing his path, he found Cal's rifle where he'd dropped it and, when Bill got back to the meadow, he found Cal sitting there, hat and jacket off and his head hung down. The drops of perspiration had started to dry on his bald scalp.

It looked like he'd been sick in the grass.

3

I'd started teaching math in the Kodiak city high school the same year Joe and Mary Bascomb moved their family to Kodiak Island, renting the vacant home across the street from me. Mary was my younger sister, and she'd been wanting to get out of Anchorage and move to Kodiak for several years. When her husband accepted a job at the Navy Base as a power plant operator, she got her wish. That fall they'd enrolled their two kids in the Kodiak schools, Janet as a sophomore in high school, Bill into the fourth grade at East Elementary, where Mary soon took a job as an aide.

I've always been an enthusiastic fisherman and hunter but Joe didn't have the patience for it. When it came time to teach Bill the rudiments of the outdoors, he suggested I might have more luck with the boy—a challenge and opportunity I couldn't refuse.

In fact, I got to know both the Bascomb children pretty well. Janet was in my first math class—a bright, serious, tenth-grade student with glasses and a quiet sort of smile that made me think she knew more than she let on. Bill was also a serious kind of lad, but how he did like to play with guns. When his folks bought him his first rifle, a single shot .22 caliber, Bill showed it off to the whole neighborhood. Mary accused me one day of being too thorough with his outdoor education—but she was smiling when she said it.

After Janet graduated from high school, she took a job as a secretary/receptionist at Kodiak Airways, the local air taxi operator. The way she tells the story, she fell in love with Charlie Doverman the day he came looking for a flying job that fall, wearing his Coast Guard aviator's dress uniform. Janet had never seen anyone so handsome.

Charlie was a lieutenant at the time, six feet tall, solidly built, blond, and good looking with a glint of aviation in his blue eyes, of far-off places, of strange languages, of space and the sea and sky and Janet fell for the whole package. He flew a UF2G for the Coast Guard, a large, twin-engined amphibian built by Grumman that all the pilots called *The Albatross*. He'd been thinking of resigning his commission to go into civil aviation anyway, and when he heard that Kodiak Airways was looking for another pilot to fly *The Goose*, a smaller amphibious aircraft also built by Grumman, he applied for the job.

The first person Charlie met at the Airways administrative office was Janet. He was still single, 26 years old and getting tired of barracks life; Charlie looked twice at the tall, slender, dark-haired receptionist with the radiant smile who escorted him in to talk to the owner. Two hours later, with the promise of a job within the next few months, Charlie took Janet to lunch; six months later they were married.

Charlie flew for the Airways for five years before he and Janet grew tired of working for someone else and decided to try something new. They'd scraped together enough money to buy an old, reconditioned Dehavilland Beaver, and with John, their two-year-old son, a dog and a cat, and all their worldly possessions, Charlie and Janet flew 140 miles northwest to Iliamna, a small bush community of less than a hundred people, where they'd also put a down payment on an old, run-down lodge on the shores of Lake Iliamna.

Bill watched them leave Kodiak with tears in his eyes. Charlie had become a hero to the teenager. I guess if it weren't for Charlie, Bill wouldn't have developed his own interest in aviation.

It was Charlie who took Bill up for his first airplane ride, a cargo run to one of the villages on the west side of the Island on a Saturday. Charlie had asked the chief pilot if he could take his brother-in-law along, and from then on Bill was hooked on flying.

I was still teaching at the high school, and found out about Bill's immediate love of flying pretty soon. He'd been just an average student until then, but when Charlie told the kid he'd have to pass some pretty tough examinations before he could get his own pilot's license, Bill's math grades started to improve—English and history, too, according to the other teachers.

After Charlie told Bill that learning to fly was expensive—$25 an hour for an airplane and instructor—Bill started looking for work. There weren't too many places that would hire a 14-year-old, but between a morning paper route and afternoons bagging groceries at Kraft's Market, Bill started to save. His ambition was to solo on his 16th birthday, the youngest age allowable under the FAA regulations—and he did.

Bill had just turned eighteen the spring he graduated from high school. From a scrawny, gangly kid, he'd matured to a solid, 180-pound six-footer. He was always busy.

When he wasn't at school or working 30 hours a week, or down at the municipal airport, he'd be off hunting somewhere. The old pickup truck he'd bought was seldom in the yard during the day; he'd leave before daylight and not return until after dark. Some nights he'd show up at my door with a few rabbits or ptarmigan or, occasionally, some venison. Although his own family didn't like to eat a lot of game, he knew I did. I'd cook it and we'd sit down to a late dinner of whatever he'd brought home.

Next to flying and hunting, I guess basketball was Bill's favorite pastime. I put up a basket and backboard against my garage door to encourage him; when Bill was home, day or night, I could hear the constant pounding of the ball on the driveway as he practiced his shooting and dribbling. In high school, Bill was the star of the team, averaging 20 points a game from his point-guard position.

I went to all his games, and was a little surprised to hear that he'd turned down a basketball scholarship at one of the small colleges in the Pacific Northwest to join the Navy. Then he explained it over a rabbit stew one night that spring: he'd already earned his private pilot's license but couldn't afford to pay for all the training needed for his commercial license and instrument rating. He could just as easily join the Air Force or Coast Guard, but he'd still need a college degree to fly for any of the military services. But he also found out that honorable service in any of the armed forces gave him access to the G.I. Bill—and that would pay for the advanced flight training he needed, or at least 90% of it. He'd thought it all out—he wanted to be a commercial pilot like Charlie. Basketball was a game; flying was a career.

Bill hadn't yet considered the possibilities of becoming a hunting guide.

• • •

After Bill closed the hunting camp, he flew John back to Iliamna in his Cessna 180 and then brought Cal to

Kodiak to put him on the next airplane headed to Anchorage. Bill hoped he'd never see the arrogant and immature millionaire again. Little did he know what the summer was about to bring.

The next week, Bill got a phone call from Janet. Usually his sister was quiet and unshakable, a strong Alaskan woman accustomed to hard work and harsh living; today she sounded distraught. "I think Charlie had a heart attack."

"When, Sis?"

"An hour ago," she said. "He was in the hangar working on the Beaver. When he didn't come in for morning coffee, John went looking for him. He was lying on the floor out there." She paused briefly to catch her breath. "Bill, I'm scared."

"Is he conscious?"

"Yes, but he says his chest feels tight."

"Have you called for a medivac?"

"John just called Anchorage. They'll be here in an hour."

The air ambulance serving almost all Alaska was a Lear Jet and, even though the flight crew was on immediate standby, it would take them 20 minutes to get airborne and another 30 minutes to get to Iliamna. They usually had a doctor on board; if not, there was always an Emergency Medical Technician on every flight. "Where's Charlie now?" Bill asked.

"Here on the sofa," Janet said. She was still breathing hard. "John and I carried him in."

John was a tough one, and his mother no slouch—Charlie weighed at least 200 pounds. "You've got to get him to the airport, Jan. Do you have any guests to help?"

"Two photographers just arrived and they said they'd help. John's making a stretcher now. We'll get Charlie to the plane on time—but he's worried about something else."

"Should have known Charlie would be worrying about something—probably business," Bill said. "What is it?" Since Charlie and Janet had left Kodiak, they'd been working their buns off for over 25 years trying to keep afloat in a sea of debt.

"The two photographers are here to film bears for a PBS special. Charlie was going to fly them around."

"Damn!" Bill said. If it weren't in the middle of the spring bear season, he could have done it himself, but he still had that last client booked for a 10-day hunt; Bill was supposed to pick him up in Anchorage in two days, then get John and take them both to camp.

If you don't live in Alaska, you can't hunt grizzlies without a guide; some of the guides doubled their income by taking a couple of hunters on a single hunt—some even took three or four—but Bill made it a rule to take only one at a time. That way they usually each got a bear and, at the price Bill had to charge, he figured they deserved his undivided attention. But that meant he wouldn't be able to help his sister out for a couple of weeks. "How about Skytaxi?" he asked her. It was a small, two-airplane air taxi operation in Iliamna. "Have you called them?"

"They've got the mail contract to all the villages this year, and for the next month they're booked up with geologists from some mining company," she said. "Bill, we need you. I need you."

Bill didn't have to think long about it; if Janet said she needed him, she needed him. He knew a guy in Anchorage who was just getting started in the guiding business and would be glad to take Bill's last client of the season—and share the fee with him just to get his foot in the door. And Bill knew Janet really didn't have anyone else. Charlie came from a family of bankers in Minnesota—they'd be about as much help around a fishing lodge as a bunch of porcupines.

It would cost him, but family came first. "Jan, you just

get Charlie to the hospital and stay there with him until he's well again," Bill said. "My 180 is still on wheels; I'll switch to floats tonight and fly over tomorrow and take care of everything—tell Charlie not to worry, the lodge will be in good hands."

Bill worked half the night removing the landing gear and mounting the floats on his airplane. At 3:00 a.m. he finally lay down and took a catnap on the old sofa in the hangar, but was up again at 7:00. By 8:30 he'd refueled and launched the floatplane; by 9:00 he was airborne headed for Afognak Island, climbing to a few hundred feet below the 4500 foot overcast. He liked to fly with a lot of altitude under him while crossing the 30 miles of ocean between Kodiak Island and the Alaska Peninsula.

At 7,000 feet above sea level, Mount Douglas had its peak in the clouds. When Bill approached the western side of Shelikof Straits, he started his descent and rounded Cape Douglas a few hundred feet above the ground. Kamishak Bay was dead ahead; its landmarks were as familiar to him as the capes, bays, and fjords of Kodiak Island.

Cape Douglas stands at the southwestern end of the bay; to the northeast looms Mt. Augustine, a volcanic island that erupts every ten years. Between them—in a giant arc more than 50 miles long—lies an uninhabited, barren, God-forsaken shoreline of black sand beaches, glacier-fed rivers, and rocky headlands towering hundreds of feet over the sea. Today it was a colorless scene—an ominous gray sky over a charcoal sea tumultuous with white foam. Bill had a 30-knot tailwind pushing him across the bay and had gotten out of Kodiak just in time—in another six hours the weather over his entire route was forecast to be unflyable, with winds over 50 knots, severe turbulence within a thousand feet of the surface, and rain, drizzle, and fog reducing visibility to less than a mile.

Kamishak Bay has a reputation among mariners and

pilots for unrelentingly foul weather—particularly during the winter—and nobody lives there for long. There'd been a native settlement at one time along the beach at the outlet of the Douglas River, but they'd abandoned it decades ago. Around the cape on the Shelikof Strait side, the navigation charts still show a village at the mouth of Big River, but Bill had walked the beach there several times in the past and never found any sign of human inhabitants, past or present.

The only evidence of man is flotsam on the littered beaches: rough logs and dimensioned timber, hatch combings, crab pot floats, fish nets, and a lot more junk washed or thrown overboard from the fishing vessels, tankers, and freighters that ply the waters around the Gulf of Alaska, Shelikof Strait, and Lower Cook Inlet. The white man was certainly affecting the environment, throwing all that stuff overboard so that wind and tide brought it ashore. And it wasn't just the white man; half of it came from Japanese, Taiwanese, and Korean fishing boats: saké bottles, glass floats, and hatch combings with oriental writing on them.

The choppy bay passed under his wings, wind-streaked and foamy and gray. It looked desolate and forbidding, but the oxygen-rich salt water throbbed with life: clams, crabs, birds, fish, seals, sea otters, sea lions, and whales, all thriving within a vibrant ecosystem. Flying low along the coast, Bill spotted several moose that had been driven from the mountain valleys by heavy snows and were now feeding on the willows and alders close to the sea. It would be June before they could climb back to their summer feeding grounds.

The flight took him close to his hunting camp, his home away from home, his little part of paradise still free from the encroachment of humans. At least it was his while he stayed there, but he knew that when he left, the animals once again took over the valley. Foxes, wolves, and wolverines would walk through his backyard all summer in their constant search for food; snowshoe hares, shrews, and mice would skitter cautiously from one hidden crevice to another searching for twigs, dried grasses, and buds for their own dinners. The big, bad, and mean would survive, the timid and weak would perish in that dog-eat-dog environment, and as he flew over the low hills behind camp he could see crisscrossing animal tracks of predator and quarry in the snow still deeply piled in the canyons.

A few minutes later he saw fresh bear tracks in the snow on the ridge behind his cabin. Was it The Warden? The sow he'd been with only a few days ago? One of his many children? Who knows? A bear that old had sired plenty of cubs, probably more than his share. Maybe that walleyed juvenile Bill had seen a few years ago was one of his; same dark chocolate color, anyway, with that lighter tan around its eyes that set him apart from the others. There were very few dark chocolate bears among the hundred or more Bill had seen over the years.

Bears. For three years John had been telling Bill about the dozens of bears he and Charlie had encountered along the salmon streams every day, all summer, while guiding sport fishermen. He'd talked about the antics of both the people and the bears when they'd faced each other across an open beach, of the confrontations, the fears and reactions, the bluffs, the false charges—but mainly the ignorance of most people and the arrogance of some when facing a bear so close you could hit it with a stone. Now it would be Bill's turn to see it—all of it. If Charlie had had a heart attack, he'd probably never fly again—the FAA would never give him his medical back—and Bill might be there all summer helping Janet out.

As a hunting guide, the bears of Alaska had been Bill's inspiration and meal ticket for years—now he'd get to see another side of them.

4

Thirty minutes later, Bill landed in the choppy bay behind Iliamna Lodge and taxied to the beach. John, in hip boots and windbreaker, was waiting to help with the plane. Bill had never seen him look so solemn.

"What happened, John?" Bill called as he stepped from the cockpit to the float.

"It's worse than we thought, Uncle Bill." He grabbed the bow of the float as the plane drifted toward the beach. "Dad had another heart attack in the hospital this morning."

"A bad one?"

"Mom said they just barely saved him."

"When does the next commercial flight leave for Anchorage?"

"Tomorrow."

"I'll take you myself," Bill said. Despite the threatening weather, it was the least he could do. "I've got enough fuel—pack a bag and introduce me to the staff; then we're off." Bill moored the plane to a stake driven into the beach and followed John up the hill to the lodge.

Mel, the head cook, was a tall gangly man in his mid-50s who wore a tall, white chef's hat whenever he was in the kitchen. His wife Liz—a short, gray-haired lady who favored loose-fitting flowered smocks and comfortable sneakers—was about the same age as her husband. Together they handled all the kitchen chores; their daughter Dorothy, a trim, pleasant woman of 30, was both housekeeper and waitress. She was married to a Coast Guardsman stationed aboard a Cutter homeported in Kodiak, currently assigned to fisheries enforcement patrol in the Bering Sea for most of the summer.

Mel handed Bill a cup of steaming coffee. "This'll hold you for a while," he said. "You want to eat something before you leave?"

Bill hadn't thought about food, but all of a sudden he was hungry. "No time to sit down now but how about some sandwiches to take along?"

"Coming right up," Mel said, disappearing back into the kitchen. Before Bill left, Mel handed him a bag of sandwiches along with a thermos and two cups.

In half an hour they were back in the air, John in the copilot's seat. After fighting moderate turbulence and 30-knot headwinds through Lake Clark Pass, they landed on Lake Hood in Anchorage two hours later.

John caught a cab to the hospital while Bill refueled. He wanted to look in on Charlie and Janet himself but the storm was approaching fast and he'd made a commitment to them to watch things. If he didn't leave immediately, it could be days before anyone could fly through the pass again. His return flight was really bumpy but all downwind and he made it back in an hour and a half.

It was 10:00 p.m. before Bill landed, but only just dusk. The two photographers were checking over the boxes of equipment they'd stacked in the main room of the lodge, stopping to follow Bill into the dining room to talk while he ate the cold supper Mel had left in the refrigerator.

Malcolm and Marilyn Foster were quite a pair. He was tall, she was short; he was muscular, a football player and wrestler in college, she was dainty, not much more than a hundred pounds; he was dark, with a heavy beard and mustache, she was a platinum blond with long hair tied in braids; his eyes scowled darkly from beneath heavy brows, her blue-green eyes sparkled as she talked. And could she talk—almost non-stop from the time Bill arrived. Malcolm said very little; when he did, he picked his words carefully—until they started talking about photography. Then they tumbled out non-stop. That slowed his wife down some, but not much.

He was 35, she was 25; they'd been married three years. They'd met in photography school, where Malcolm had been a teacher and she his brightest student. They hadn't dated until she'd graduated; that's what she said, anyway.

Marilyn continued their life history as if it were imperative to impress Bill with their credentials. Malcolm had been a nature photographer for ten years before they'd met. Forming a husband and wife team, they'd started with stills, Malcolm's primary interest, then expanded into video, Marilyn's preference. As a team, she emphasized, they were building a reputation in wildlife video production and that's why they'd been given this job.

The Public Broadcasting Station in Boston had given them the assignment: photograph grizzly bears in Alaska. They'd traveled a long way and Charlie, low bidder on the contracts for both lodging and transportation, had promised them he could provide just what they needed.

"We want to see the bears in their own habitat,"

Marilyn instructed. "We want to see where they live, how they live, what they eat, how they interact with each other, everything."

"From the air?" Bill asked.

"On the ground," she insisted. She certainly did monopolize the conversation; Malcolm hadn't said two words since Bill started eating. "We'll want some aerial shots for background, but most of the filming has to be done on the ground and up close."

"Close?" Bill didn't much like the sound of that. "How close?"

"As close as we can get."

"A hundred yards?"

"Fifty feet."

"Go back to the zoo," Bill told her. "Nobody's safe that close to a wild grizzly."

"Says who?" she demanded, eyes flashing.

"Says me," Bill told her.

"So who are you?"

Bill didn't even bother to answer. The woman was beginning to get on his nerves.

"John told me that Bill's been a bear guide for 20 years," Malcolm said.

She looked at Bill incredulously, then turned to her husband. "He hunts them?"

"To hunt them, you have to know where they are," Bill pointed out, taking his dishes into the kitchen before he slugged the damn woman. Hell's bells, first Charlie has a heart attack, then Bill has to give up a paying customer to help, now he has to put up with this impudent little do-gooder who probably never saw a live grizzly outside a zoo.

"He's right," Malcolm said. "If he hunts them, he should know where to find them." Bill didn't hear what she said next, he was slamming the dishes around in the stainless steel sink. "Can we start tomorrow?" Malcolm called.

Bill glanced out the window. The storm that threatened that morning had finally arrived. Through the rain-spattered glass he watched six-foot waves crash against the beach—thank God Charlie had built his airplane moorings in the sheltered bay behind the lodge. In that surf, they'd be scrap aluminum in minutes.

"We'll start when this storm passes through," Bill called back through the open door. "Don't set your alarm clock—I'll get you up if we can fly."

Malcolm got an earful before he got to bed—Marilyn was still fuming about being told to go back to the zoo to see grizzlies up close. After her husband finally dropped off to sleep, she set her alarm clock.

The rain had stopped by morning, but a three-hundred-foot ceiling of dark stratus clouds kept them grounded. Fortunately, the wind had shifted from southeast to south and started to diminish, a sign of better weather ahead. Bill explained the weather patterns at breakfast, but it was a waste of breath; Marilyn asked when they could leave every half hour all morning anyway. When the sun finally peeked through a break in the clouds and quickly disappeared again, she ran to find Bill one more time.

"How about now?" she asked, pointing to the sky. The stratus layer had definitely thinned and the sun was faintly visible through a film of running scud. "Can you fly in the sunshine?"

"We'll start after lunch," Bill said, "but wait a minute, ma'am. Who are you trying to impress with your sarcasm? Me or Malcolm?"

Marilyn flipped her long hair and silently stalked across the room. Glancing toward the kitchen door, Bill called after her, "Tell Malcolm that Mel's ready to serve." When Bill entered the dining room two minutes later, they were both sitting at the table.

Bill planned the first flight to show them the lay of the land, so they could get some aerial shots for background if the light was right. "One word of advice," he said as they boarded the airplane. "Things happen fast out there, so be ready."

"What do you mean, be ready?" Marilyn asked.

"Keep your cameras ready," Bill said. "Keep your eyes open. Be ready."

"You just fly the plane," she said. "You don't have to worry about us—we're always ready."

Bill climbed into the pilot's seat, started the engine, and taxied into the bay, the Cessna 180 rolling in the swells left from the night's storm. Both passengers watched him go through the pre-flight check-off, Malcolm from the copilot's seat on his right and Marilyn from the right rear seat. He'd placed them on the same side so that when they saw something, he could bank the plane so that they could both photograph it easily.

"Either of you ever flown in a small plane before?" Bill asked.

"It's as safe as driving a car," Marilyn shouted from behind him.

He should have expected that—of course she'd have the last word. After a final check to see that they'd fastened their seat belts—"Of course we have"—he pushed the throttle full forward for take-off power. The roar of the engine drowned out all other conversation from the back seat—sweet relief, although short-lived. When he climbed to an altitude of a thousand feet over Lake Iliamna and reduced both throttle and propeller speed to cruise, Marilyn picked up right where she'd left off. Bill kept his noise-deadening headphones on and pretended he couldn't hear her.

For the next three hours, they flew over all the places where Bill thought they might see a bear, but they didn't see so much as a bear track. Finally Marilyn tapped him on the shoulder and he turned around to look at her.

"I thought you said you knew where the bears were,"

she shouted over the engine's roar.

They were flying over Kamishak Bay—he'd saved it for last. Patches of fog drifted upward on a gentle breeze from the sea as they flew over the coastline. Winter's grip had finally lost to the persuasion of spring. Now in the third week in May, the alders and willows had started to leaf, sending green shoots from the dull gray bark. Melting snows filled the mountain streams to overflowing, splashing and bubbling over rocks already worn smooth from centuries of past spring floods.

Bill followed the coastline from Cape Douglas to the McNeil River, then turned north, following the Paint River toward the pass leading inland. The sea mist broke up along the ridgeline, and they could see the undulating crests and canyons between Kamishak Bay and Lake Iliamna. Banking steeply, he circled one of the canyons for a better look. Directly below them in the snow was a bear trail that looked so fresh it sparkled in the sunshine. Bill decided to follow it.

The foot-wide track led uphill into a steep snow-clogged canyon where several small avalanches had tumbled snow toward the brushy hollow. When they saw the trail end in a hole halfway up the side of the hill, Bill knew they'd been tracking it backward.

They hadn't found the bear—they'd found where it had spent the winter. Since it was already late in May, Bill suspected it was a female, probably with a couple of cubs. Diving low over the den, he pointed out the three sets of tracks in the snow—one big set and two sets of little ones that they hadn't been able to see from a thousand feet up.

The tracks were very fresh, with sunshine glistening off the small ridges of snow around each print. They were made that morning; last night's rain would have washed out older tracks. Circling back over the ridge where they'd first seen the tracks, Bill crisscrossed back and forth following the bear's trail off the snowy ridge, through several alder and willow thickets, finally out onto a large grassy meadow only half a mile from the sea.

A medium-sized sow of about 600 pounds was feeding in the meadow. Two very small cubs—no more than 20 pounds apiece—were playing nearby: standing up and batting at each other with their paws, chasing each other around in the grass, rolling and tumbling like puppies.

From their vantage point 800 feet above them, Bill also spotted his old nemesis, The Warden, on the same hillside. The boar was creeping like a cat, sneaking along the edge of the alders with his belly close to the ground; he didn't even look up at the plane. Within 50 yards of the sow, the monster boar broke clear of the alders and charged across the open meadow.

The sow wheeled on her hind legs and sprinted to place herself between the boar and her cubs. Roaring her defiance, the sow stood her ground while the cubs scampered toward the nearest line of brush.

The whole thing didn't take 30 seconds, time enough to turn a full circle in the air. Before Bill had returned to his original heading, the sow had already been bowled over twice and was limping badly as she struggled after The Warden. Racing across the clearing, he caught one of the cubs and killed it with a single blow across its back.

The wounded sow stopped about a hundred feet from the boar and looked at him. He had one front foot resting on the small lump of fur at his feet; from his stance, and a deep growl that came from the depths of his massive chest, he dared the sow to try and take it away from him. After a few seconds, the sow turned away to follow her other cub into the alders.

As she disappeared, Bill dove the plane at The Warden, the engine screaming under full power as they passed only a few feet over his head. The old devil stood up on his back legs—with the dead cub between his feet—and swung at the plane with his front paws.

After Bill climbed back to a safer altitude, Malcolm and Marilyn filmed The Warden as he picked up the cub in his jaws and carried it into the alders.

Later, back at the lodge, Marilyn was strangely silent. Mel had prepared a delicious dinner of barbecued moose ribs, boiled potatoes, green beans, and a carrot-raisin salad that Malcolm and Bill hungrily devoured, but Marilyn barely touched hers.

"Why did that big bear kill the cub?" she finally asked, pushing the food around on her plate.

"Food," Bill answered—it was true, but there were other possible reasons. The big boar was also reducing his future competition for food, territory, and—if it was a male cub—the favors of a female during mating season. This was all theory, of course—and Bill certainly didn't want to encourage Marilyn to start theorizing. She already had enough to say about everything else.

"He'll actually eat that poor little thing?"

"I told you grizzlies are mean when they're hungry."

"That's not what the books say," Marilyn said. "There were pictures of bears feeding only 50 feet apart, both sexes, and cubs."

"That's later in the summer," Bill told her. "The rivers are full of salmon then, so there's plenty of food for all of them."

"That's right," Marilyn turned to her husband. "The major difference between the grizzlies that live along the coast and those that live up in the mountains is size, and that's because the coastal bears eat so much salmon in the summer."

Now she was lecturing them both about bears. Bill wondered how Malcolm put up with her.

"But they both carry the same scientific name," Marilyn continued, "Ur*sus* (bear), *arctos* (brown), *horribilis* (grizzly). Some of the coastal boars, like your Warden, can grow to 1500 pounds, while the inland boars seldom reach more than half that."

Bill started to say, "He's not *my* Warden, he's *The* Warden," but she wasn't to be denied her audience. She'd been storing up all these words for three hours in the plane.

"The bears living on Kodiak, Afognak, and Shuyak Islands carry a different sub-species classification, *Ursus arctos middendorfi*."

"On Kodiak they're called Kodiak bears," Bill said. "Around here and on the Alaska Peninsula they're called brown bears. To me they're all grizzlies." He picked up his plate and headed for the kitchen.

5

Bill might have enjoyed a quiet cup of coffee after dinner but Marilyn was not to be denied. The day's events were too much on her mind—and what was on her mind was automatically shared with those unfortunate enough to be within earshot.

Malcolm and Bill were sitting in the lounge, neither of them saying very much. A 15-knot southwesterly breeze had sprung up, dissipating the last of the storm clouds and replacing them with lightly billowing, white cumulus puffs, a sure sign of good weather for the next few days.

Then Marilyn walked into the lounge carrying her own cup of coffee and sat down opposite Bill on the sofa. "Why did it take you so long to find those bears today?" she demanded.

"It's too early to see many bears," Bill said. "We were lucky today."

"Charlie said we'd see lots of bears!"

"In a few weeks you will." Bill knew what Charlie'd probably said; he also knew why he'd said it. Like almost everything else, it was simple economics. May is a slow month at a fishing lodge. When the salmon runs start in June, he'd have plenty of guests; right now he needed the business to pay his bills—which don't wait for the salmon.

"But Charlie promised…"

"Bears aren't stupid," Bill tried to deflect her. "Right now it's hunting season. In hunting season bears can be harder than hell to find."

"You mean to sit there and tell me they know it's hunting season?" Marilyn flipped her spoon in the air as if now she'd heard everything.

No one could tell that woman anything. Bill changed the subject. "We've got some minus tides coming up," he said, turning to Malcolm. "Want to go clam digging?"

"No!" Marilyn slammed her fist down on the table. "We want to see bears!"

"I've seen bears eat clams," Bill said.

"Sure—on the half-shell, or fried?" Marilyn scoffed.

"What the hell," Malcolm said, putting down his cup. "You want to go dig clams, we'll go dig clams." He stood up and stomped upstairs to bed.

It took Bill most of the next day to put the Cessna back on wheels so they could land on the beach. The following morning he told Mel where they were going and to plan on serving razor clams for dinner that evening. When Mel asked how to cook them, Bill almost threw a pot at him.

"I thought you were a cook!" he shouted. "Call Janet if you can't figure it out for yourself."

Bill stamped out, then three minutes later went back into the kitchen. "I'm sorry, Mel, but that woman is getting on my nerves," he said. "Don't bother Janet; she has enough to worry about. If you've never cooked razors before, you'll probably need help cleaning them, too. I'll show you how when we get back." Mel was smiling again when Bill left.

Low tide was at 9:37 a.m. In order to arrive on the beach an hour before the low, they left Iliamna just before 8:00 and landed on one of the beaches around Kamishak Bay by 8:30. The sand was hard and smooth; it made a runway five miles long and 300 yards wide. Only the small tail wheel of the Cessna dug into the sand; the two main tires rode as high on the firm surface as they had on the packed gravel of Charlie's runway.

It was dead calm; the sea lay as flat as the beach. The half-foot swells, generated from somewhere in the cold North Pacific, curled slightly, then slid up the sand without breaking. A bright sun was slowly dissipating a thin morning fog that lay over the water, and they could see every hill, ridge, and mountain between Mt. Douglas to the southeast and the 10,000-foot peak of Mt. Iliamna to the north. A brilliant blue sky outlined the snow-capped mountains; the browns and grays of the surrounding hills showed off the new greens of the alder and willow thickets crowding the edges of the sand.

Malcolm, Marilyn, and Bill were alone on a beach that appeared to stretch around the bay in one unbroken arc. As they climbed out of the aircraft into a world of silence, only the distant lament of a passing gull penetrated the quiet. Even Marilyn started whispering as she and Malcolm unloaded their cameras, tripods, and bags of film and lenses.

Taking the clam shovel and two 20-gallon buckets from the baggage compartment, Bill started walking toward the water. With his eyes on the sand, he was looking for the telltale dimple that showed where a razor clam had stuck his neck out.

The tide was still falling. Fifty feet from the water's edge Bill spotted the first dimple, a quarter-inch hole surrounded by a narrow doughnut of loose sand. Dropping the shovel and buckets, he took off his jacket and rolled up the right sleeve of his shirt. As he bent down to start digging, Malcolm and Marilyn hurried over to watch.

There aren't any rocks or stones on a razor clam beach—just sand—and the clams move up and down through the sand using a powerful digger (called, appropriately, a foot) that can slip them along at five to six inches a minute, sometimes faster. Occasionally they're fairly close to the surface, but most of the time the clams are at least a foot down in the sand.

Razor clam holes tend to slant toward the water, so Bill started digging about six inches seaward of the dimple. He quickly dug a hole a foot deep. The clam shovel has a short handle and a long, narrow blade that's curved to dig deep and fast. As water from the surrounding sand started seeping into the hole, Bill dropped the shovel, knelt down, and reached in with his right hand, digging with the tips of his fingers until he felt the top of the shell. With a firm grip and steady pull, he slowly eased the one-pound delicacy out of the sand.

The thin brown shells of these clams are streaked with shades of tan; they measure about eight inches long, three inches wide, and over an inch thick. When they're fat, as they always were on this beach, part of the beige-colored meat sticks out between the halves of their shells. After Bill had dug another half-dozen, Malcolm asked if he could try. Bill gave him the shovel.

"Here's another one, Malcolm," Marilyn said, wandering past them, "and another, and another—wow, they're all over the place!" Working together, with Malcolm digging and his wife spotting, they filled the first bucket in 30 minutes while Bill stood and watched.

Standing there daydreaming, Bill almost missed seeing

the sow and her year-old cub step out of the brush. They were less than a quarter of a mile away.

"Company, Malcolm," Bill said.

"I didn't hear another plane come in," Marilyn said, not bothering to look up. She'd really gotten into clam digging and was down on her knees with one arm buried in a hole. "Darn, some of these clams are deep."

"They didn't come in a plane," Bill said.

"Don't be ridiculous, Bill," she said, proudly drawing the clam out of the hole. She still hadn't looked up. "We would have heard them."

"Bears don't make much noise," he said. That made her look up quick enough.

By now the tide had fallen way beneath its normal low range and exposed hundreds of acres of sand usually covered by salt water. The sow, a typical tannish-brown coastal grizzly about 600 pounds, slowly walked out on the freshly exposed beach. As she picked up each front foot and flopped it, heel first, down in front of her, Bill recognized Carlotta. She'd had two cubs when Bill had dug clams there last spring, but he wasn't surprised that she only had a single now, since only two-thirds of the cubs survive their first year. But that particular pigeon-toed dance was unmistakable, and Carlotta was the name of a dancer he'd seen in a movie once. It seemed to fit.

Carlotta was studying the ground directly in front of her. Near the water's edge, she saw the small telltale squirt of a razor clam starting to dig its way deeper under the surface. Pouncing on the spot, she dug like a dog. With powerful strokes of her front legs, she quickly scooped a big hole where the dimple had been. The hapless clam came flying out with the sand.

"My God, the cameras!" Marilyn cried. "Get the cameras!" She and Malcolm jumped to their feet and ran up the beach for their equipment.

It took Bill half-a-minute to dig each clam; Carlotta

took five seconds—the bigger boars took even less. The cub sat down and watched its mother eat the first clam. Sand, juice, and fragments of shell dripped from her powerful jaws as she turned her head to look up and down the beach.

She knew the humans were there—probably knew before she even stepped onto the beach—but it didn't seem to bother her much, perhaps because they were so far away. Swallowing the one-pound morsel, she started her slow walk down the beach again, the cub following along behind.

Bill watched her eat three more clams before sharing one with the cub. By that time Malcolm had his camera set up on a tripod; he was using a telephoto lens for close-ups while Marilyn walked around with her camera on her shoulder for longer shots. Bill was about to go back to clam digging when another bear walked onto the beach, a boar he immediately recognized. He was much closer to them— only a hundred yards away.

"I call the sow Carlotta, Malcolm," Bill said, "and that new one to your left is Walleye." Malcolm's head swiveled with the camera he was using, never taking his eye off the lens. His face was a wrinkle of smiles—he'd finally found what he'd come for. The closer bear must have half-filled the 500-millimeter telephoto lens he was using.

Bill had seen Walleye on this same beach four years ago with his mother and another cub. That would make him five years old now—big enough to be a threat but not old enough to gain all the wisdom he'd need for a full life. Walleye started toward the water's edge, moving closer to them.

"It's getting a little crowded," Bill announced. "We'd better move back toward the plane."

Malcolm didn't argue; he pulled up his tripod, stuck it under one arm, hefted the camera onto his other shoulder, and slowly backed off, filming as he went. Marilyn, of course, was another story.

"Get out of the way," she ordered, when Bill walked over and stood in front of her camera. She was so intent on tracking the mother and cub that she didn't even take her eye from the eyepiece.

"You can film from the plane," Bill said. The sow was still far enough away, but Walleye was now headed straight for them.

"Get lost!" she yelled. The stupid woman didn't seem to realize that bears were the biggest predators in this country—they expect everything else to get out of their way. It was Bill's job to see that she learned it. Fast!

"Now!" He reached out and put his hand over the lens of her camera.

That got her attention. "What the hell do you think you're doing?" She jerked the camera away.

"Move, lady!" Bill yelled back, pointing to Walleye coming up behind them. "Unless you intend to fight that bear for this clam bed!"

Then she saw Walleye—he was little over a hundred feet away—but she wasn't about to back off. Instead, she swung around to start filming the boar, oblivious of the danger she was putting them all in. Bill grabbed her around her waist and carried her, camera and all, kicking and screaming up the beach.

"She's your wife," he told Malcolm, dumping her on the sand at his feet. "You talk some sense into her."

Marilyn looked mad enough to choke on it. Her face was contorted in rage, her blue eyes mere slits under quivering lashes. "So you're the big brave bear guide!" she jeered. "If that bear was so dangerous, why didn't you just shoot it?"

"Stow it!" Malcolm shouted. "We've got bears to film. I'll cover this one—you get the mother and cub."

Marilyn may have been a first-class bitch with Bill, but she snapped right to when Malcolm cracked the whip.

Walleye walked to the clam bed they'd just left. Search and dig, search and dig, the 600-pound boar was as adept at finding clams as Carlotta, who was almost his size. With her cub in trail, she slowly made her way down the beach toward the young male. As she approached, still pausing every minute or so to dig another clam, Walleye moved away. He always left at least a hundred feet between them; teenager or not, he knew enough to stay away from a sow with a cub.

After watching its mother for half an hour, the cub started to copy her, eventually finding its own clam holes. The 200-pound sibling couldn't dig as fast as its mother and didn't get many clams, but they could all see that it'd gotten the idea.

By the time the tide changed, Malcolm and Marilyn had taken all the film they wanted and they took off for Iliamna with their bucket of clams, leaving the three bears still digging. The beach had so many potholes in it, it looked like a battlefield.

"What a mess," Marilyn said, the camera at her eye again.

"In another hour you won't see a thing," Bill shouted over the roar of the engine. The incoming tide would fill up all the holes with sand so that the beach would look as smooth tomorrow as it had that morning.

"How long will the bears be there?" Malcolm asked when they got back to the lodge. He and Marilyn had unloaded their equipment and were just going upstairs to wash up before dinner.

"As long as the minus tides last," Bill said. "It's easy pickings for them." If there's one thing Bill had learned about bears in the past 20 years, it's that they always flock to easy pickings.

"Will we go back tomorrow?" Malcolm asked.

Bill knew that they already had enough clams for a dozen dinners. "I've got something better to show you."

"Better?" Marilyn stopped with one foot on the steps. "Yesterday you couldn't find bear one, today we had three on the beach with us and, already, you've got something better?"

"You don't have to go," Bill said. "Malcolm can handle it."

"Come on, Marilyn," Malcolm called wearily. Bill didn't know if it was the clam digging, or the bears, or his wife, but Malcolm's indomitable spirit had faded, and he trudged heavily up the stairs.

"The hell with you, too," Marilyn said, following her husband.

Bill had spotted a dead whale floating in Kamishak Bay on the flight back. From the air, It had looked like a Beluga, a small white whale about 15 feet long that weighed about a ton. It might have been dead a day or a week, drifting with the tidal currents. By that night, the rising east wind would drive it ashore; by tomorrow the high tide would carry it further up the beach.

There's nothing that draws bears faster than a big, rotting, stinking whale carcass.

6

After spotting the whale, Bill had made a low pass over the shoreline where he figured the carcass would drift ashore. He'd noticed a low bluff overlooking the beach; behind the bluff and running parallel to it lay a long sandy shelf where he could land. He figured that if they set up their camp on the shelf, Malcolm and Marilyn could film from the bluff hidden from the bears below. It was an ideal set-up; Bill couldn't have asked for a better spot.

The first thing Bill did was call John; he was going to need his help with the camp. Charlie had recovered enough to be moved out of intensive care, and was scheduled for bypass surgery in a few days. John was just as happy to get away from the oppressive air of the hospital for a while and caught the commercial flight out of Anchorage the next day. Bill filled him in as they drove to the lodge, including his opinion of Marilyn.

"She seemed real nice to me," was all John said.

"Wait till you know her better," Bill told him, easing the truck into the driveway at the lodge.

Four hours later, Bill and John were circling over the dead whale in the Cessna. It had drifted ashore right where Bill thought it would; two bears had already found it and were feeding ravenously, tearing large chunks of blubber from the carcass with their teeth. When Bill landed on the sand-blow behind the bluff, it was just as he'd suspected; the beach lay 10 to 12 feet below them. An enormous pile of driftwood had been washed up almost against the bluff, and they would be able to watch the bears feed on the whale from behind it.

After unloading, Bill returned to Iliamna to pick up the photographers and a second load of gear, leaving John to set up camp. When they returned an hour later, John already had two tents up and a stack of firewood collected, with a pot of coffee boiling on an open fire. Bill took a pair of sand anchors from the baggage compartment and screwed them into the ground, tying each wing down to an anchor of its own. He knew how strong the wind could blow across Kamishak Bay.

"Will the weather hold?" Marilyn asked John. The sky was a mantle of thick gray clouds hiding the tops of the hills. There was little wind behind the bluff where they'd landed, but it was blowing about 15 knots parallel to the beach; they could hear the surf pounding from a distant storm that was sending continuous lines of swells crashing against the shore.

"Hope so," John answered. "Don't know if we'll get much sun though."

"We don't need sunshine," she said, and went on to explain that they could get better color without the sun.

"The contrast between bright sunlight and the shadows it creates causes problems for a photographer. We prefer to have the same light intensity over our entire subject."

"John, I could use some help here," Bill called. His nephew had enough on his plate right now without that woman and her wiles. And he had a plane to unload.

"What's in those cans?" Marilyn asked as Bill hefted the first of two 16-gallon containers out of the baggage compartment and handed it to John.

"Food," John said. "The cans are supposed to be bear-proof. They're also supposed to keep the smells inside so the bears stay outside."

"And do they?"

"Usually," John said. He caught Bill's eye and didn't expand to say that when a bear really wanted to get into a food cache of any kind, it was usually successful—they don't get as large as they do on trepidation or timidity!

As soon as they'd unloaded the plane, Bill guided Malcolm to the bluff where he started setting up his camera with a telephoto lens. The lookout was even better than they'd expected. They were only a hundred feet from the whale but elevated enough to get a clear view of the entire beach. As long as they kept their heads down, the driftwood screened them from sight. Marilyn soon joined them with her own camera and tripod.

"The wind's backing to the east," Bill told Malcolm. The pungent odor of rancid meat and blubber had already reached them. "It'll blow that smell back over the land. There could be a dozen bears here by morning."

Malcolm only smiled.

Walleye and Cassius, another boar Bill and John had identified and named a few years ago, were feeding on the whale. Cassius was a year or two older than Walleye. That would put his weight close to 750 pounds. Another few years and he'd make a nice trophy for some hunter.

There was no telling how long they'd been on the

beach, but Walleye had already developed a potbelly from eating blubber. Suddenly, Walleye and Cassius stopped feeding and reared up on their hind legs to look northward up the shoreline.

A sow stepped out of the line of driftwood onto the beach a few hundred yards away, two small cubs tumbling onto the sand behind her. She was a tall rangy female with a scraggly look about her that Bill recognized at once. He called her Miss Paine after his fourth-grade teacher, another tall, rangy female who'd terrorized everyone around her—at least the kids.

Miss Paine weighed about 700 pounds, and walked slowly toward the whale, her cubs in trail. When she was halfway to the carcass, she stopped and reared up on her hind feet. She only stood a few seconds but her message was clear. As soon as she started walking toward the whale again, the two boars trotted down the beach to the right of the watchers, each of them looking back to check on the sow. Miss Paine had it all to herself.

"Just like that?" Marilyn asked. "Two of them and they give up that easily?"

"They didn't give up," John answered, pointing down the beach. "See—they're just waiting until she leaves."

So they were. Walleye was seated a hundred yards away scratching himself under the chin with a hind foot. Cassius was lying down with his head resting on his outstretched front paws. Both bears were still watching the whale—and the sow.

An hour later Miss Paine suddenly stopped feeding and reared up on her own hind feet. Another sow had shown up, this one with a single yearling cub. Carlotta, one of Miss Paine's daughters from several years ago, was now all grown up and ready to take on the world.

The 15-knot sea breeze had started a ripple of small waves dancing over each larger swell. The 2,000-foot overcast of gray clouds drifted shoreward on the wind, bringing with it a slight mist that rapidly fogged their glasses. Malcolm and Marilyn frequently cleaned their camera lenses as the two sows faced each other only 50 yards apart, their cubs huddled behind their respective mothers. Walleye and Cassius stood up and watched.

The two sows were almost the same size, although Miss Paine was the heavier; weight, age, and experience favored Miss Paine, youth and enthusiasm Carlotta. The fact that they were mother and daughter didn't seem to affect them; they acted like strangers.

First Miss Paine reared up on her hind legs, then Carlotta; neither one made a sound. Then both dropped back on all fours and stood staring at each other. Carlotta slowly took a few steps toward the whale, her single cub close behind her; after she'd covered 20 feet or so, she stopped and reared up again, her cub also standing on its hind feet. This time Miss Paine didn't bother.

Step by step, Carlotta continued her slow and deliberate approach, her large head low to the sand and swinging back and forth with the movement of her front shoulders and legs. Her large hind quarters swayed with each step, her large whitened claws poking five holes in the sand in front of each footprint. Neither Bill nor John could tell if she and Miss Paine recognized each other or not. When they were only 25 feet from each other—with the dead whale directly between them—Carlotta stopped again. The two sows stared over the bloated belly of the whale at each other for a full 30 seconds; then, both sows started to feed, one at the head and the other near the tail. The cubs sat down to wait.

"So far they don't seem to know we're here," Bill whispered to Malcolm who was crouched nearby. Marilyn and John were 50 feet away, crouching behind another log half buried in the sand. "The wind is still blowing from them to us."

"Would it make any difference if it did?"

"Probably not, but you never know." Glancing at his watch, Bill saw it was already 10:00 p.m. "Dinner time," he said, and waved to John, pointing at his watch and then back to camp.

Malcolm looked at his own watch in surprise. "Seems like we just got here."

"Six hours passes pretty quickly out here sometimes," Bill responded.

"Is there any reason we can't leave our equipment set up here?" Malcolm asked John as he and Marilyn joined them. "So we can get an early start in the morning?"

"I wouldn't," John said.

"Why not?"

"Bears are curious. If one comes along this way, he'll be sure to investigate."

"So they investigate, so what?" Marilyn said.

"Bears are also opportunists," Bill said. "And they're used to ripping things apart to get at what's inside."

"Like tents?" Marilyn said—but Bill could see she didn't believe a word of it. But Malcolm had more sense; he wasn't about to take chances with their expensive equipment, and they brought it with them to camp.

John had set up two small sleeping tents and one larger one for cooking. His campfire was at the focus of a semicircle formed by the three tents. The fire had gone out while they were on the beach, but he quickly started another with some newspaper and kindling he'd gathered earlier.

As they stood silently chewing a quick supper of sandwiches and potato salad washed down with hot tea, a bird flew over the camp and perched on the top of the cook tent.

"There's one I haven't seen before," Marilyn said. "What kind of bird is that, John?"

"A Canada Jay," John answered. "Some people call it a gray jay, others call it a camp robber."

"Camp robber?" Marilyn and Malcolm said in unison.

"Yeah," John said. "They show up wherever we camp and beg for scraps."

The fluffy bird was slightly bigger than a robin and had a gray back and a white breast and throat. The black patch across the back of its head and white forehead suggested an oversized chickadee. Bill and John had seen them at almost every campsite they'd ever used throughout the state. They eat anything, from bread crusts to the fat scraped off the inside of a bear's hide. When Marilyn tossed a piece of Mel's homemade bread onto the ground near the tent, the jay swooped down, picked it up in its short, black bill, and flew away.

"Ooooh," Marilyn said. "Where'd it go?" Her face was radiant, her smile genuine, her interest infectious as she followed the bird's flight until it dipped over the dune and out of sight. She'd already filmed the birds around the whale carcass and commented on their numbers: 50 or more gulls, a dozen ravens, four magpies, and a pair of bald eagles.

A minute later the jay returned with an empty bill and perched on the tent again.

"He couldn't have eaten that so quickly," Marilyn observed.

"He didn't," John said. "He hid it in that patch of spruce trees behind the airplane."

"That's why we call them camp robbers," Bill said. "He'll do that all night until we run out of food." Bill finished his plate, drained the last of his tea, and dropped the dishes into the pan of water John had heating beside the fire.

"Give me another piece of bread, John," Marilyn said. "That bird looks hungry."

John handed her the bag. Fifteen minutes later, when the three men crawled into their sleeping bags, Marilyn was still feeding the jay.

When Bill got up five hours later, the first thing he

noticed was fresh bear tracks leading right through the middle of camp. John saw them and whistled. "I didn't hear a thing, did you?"

"Hear what?" Malcolm asked, crawling from the low entrance of the tent John had set up for the photographers. His long dark hair was tousled and he was rubbing sleep from his eyes. "Are they what I think they are?" he said, looking down at the tracks.

"From the size," John said, "I'd say it was probably Walleye."

Bill bent down to measure the length of the hind foot. His hand span from thumb to little finger was nine inches; the track measured about two inches shy of a full span, making its foot seven inches long from the heel to the front of the pad behind the toes. "It's a seven-footer, all right" Bill said.

"What do you mean a seven-footer?" Marilyn asked, her long blond hair sticking out from under a scarf.

John explained it. "We measure the length of the hide from nose to tail, and the width across the front legs, then add them together and divide by two," he said. "The measurement of the hind foot in inches is about the same as the square measurement of the hide in feet."

Bill didn't think she believed him, but Malcolm had already gone for his camera and was stooped over following and filming the tracks through camp. In the half-light of a cloudy dawn, Marilyn walked over to watch.

Behind the bluff where they'd camped, the wind was calm, though laden with moisture, and the tent flys had droplets running off them. The sand was wet and dark beneath their boots. The nearby green hills were hazy but visible; the higher mountains disappeared in the mist. The air tasted salty; they couldn't see the bay, but they could still hear the surf pounding on the beach.

John quickly had a fire going and started a pot of coffee while Bill walked over to the airplane; it was their only way out of there, and he checked it for airworthiness every morning. Fifteen minutes later John called them to breakfast and handed them bowls of dry granola and raisins. At least the coffee and the milk for their cereal was hot.

"What, no bacon and eggs this morning?" Marilyn complained, then took her bowl of cereal and walked to the nearest log and sat down to eat alone.

Malcolm stood around the fire with John and Bill and quietly munched away, glancing toward the beach every few minutes. He looked anxious to get started, so as soon as the two photographers had finished, Bill led them back to the bluff. "Join us as soon as you clean up here, John," he said.

Miss Paine and Carlotta were still stationed at opposite ends of the carcass, with their cubs close by and also feeding. Carlotta's yearling cub was tearing chunks out of the blubber by itself; Miss Paine's two small 25-pound cubs were chewing on pieces she'd ripped off and dropped on the sand for them. Walleye and Cassius had moved much closer; from the looks of their distended stomachs, they'd both gorged themselves sometime during the night.

The bears had torn open the stomach cavity and scattered the entrails along the beach. The wind was still blowing from the sea toward the watchers, bringing the now over-ripe smell of rotting blubber and guts directly to them. It was almost enough to make Bill sick, although Malcolm didn't seem to mind it. When John joined them a few minutes later, Marilyn tied her scarf around the lower part of her face to keep out the worst of the stench. It was apparent she was feeling sick even if she'd never admit it. John suggested the smell might not be as bad down on the beach; they seemed to be getting the worst of it up on the bluff.

"Go ahead," Bill told him. "Just make sure you keep her behind the driftwood. The bears don't seem to know we're here, and I'd like to keep it that way."

John jumped down on the beach and turned to help Marilyn with the camera. They had to crouch a little to keep their heads below the top of the driftwood. When Bill was satisfied they weren't in any immediate danger, he went back to Malcolm.

"Where are all the big bears?" Malcolm asked.

"Six to seven hundred pounds isn't big enough?"

"You know what I mean—the really big ones."

Just then, Miss Paine and Carlotta reared up and stood looking at a spot in the line of brush farther up the beach. When their mothers stood, all three cubs stood up, too, as an enormous, chocolate-brown bear walked out of the brush, picked his way through the jungle of driftwood, and stepped onto the beach. He was twice as big as the sows.

"Big enough?" Bill said.

"Holy shit!" Malcolm whispered. "How big is it?"

"Well over a thousand pounds. Could be as much as 1200."

The Warden stood up to get a better look; both sows stood still watching him. As he dropped back on all fours, the huge boar turned sideways as if to show the other bears just how big he was. Then he turned back to the sows and snapped his jaws together several times. The sound ricocheted down the beach like rapid-fire pistol shots.

As The Warden started walking slowly toward the whale, both sows and all three cubs left, trotting down the beach a hundred feet away. Walleye and Cassius moved farther away to keep their distance from the sows; they all sat down to wait their turn.

Then Bill saw Marilyn—standing on the beach. She'd run along behind the line of driftwood and come out about 50 feet from the whale, filming the process of challenge and defeat played out on the beach by the bears.

She'd surprised them—one thing you never want to do with bears, and they'd all turned to look at her, even The Warden. Where was John? Bill glanced in all directions and couldn't find him anywhere. It didn't look like he was even on the beach. Then Bill saw him come running from the camp.

Grabbing his rifle, Bill jumped off the bluff and ran around the driftwood onto the beach himself. "Marilyn!" he shouted, running toward her. "Get back! Get off the beach!"

Now the bears turned and looked at Bill.

Just then, John came crashing through the brush onto the sand behind Bill. That was too much for the bears. The two sows tore off one way, galloping down the beach with their cubs racing along behind, while Walleye and Cassius ran back through the driftwood and up on the bluff a hundred yards from Malcolm.

Only The Warden stood his ground. Rearing up, his barrel-sized head towered five feet over Bill's, and his small black eyes stared straight at him. Bill jacked a shell into the chamber of his rifle, and slowly walked toward Marilyn—and the monarch guarding the whale.

"Back up," Bill told her softly. "Slowly, Marilyn, slowly back up."

"Don't tell me what to do!"

Then Bill heard it—the most ominous sound in bear country. The Warden was clacking his teeth together.

"Now!" He shouted, shoving her behind him. With one bound, the bear jumped over the whale carcass and charged up the beach at them.

"Whoa, bear!" Bill brought the rifle to his shoulder. "Back off, Marilyn," he said over his other shoulder, keeping his eyes on the bear. "John, get her the hell out of here!"

The Warden covered half the distance between them in a few seconds. "Whoa, bear," Bill said again.

The Warden stopped—he was only 30 feet away. One more step and Bill would have had to pull the trigger.

"Okay, Warden, the beach is yours," Bill said, keeping

his voice quiet and steady as he slowly backed away. "Eat all you want; we're leaving."

The bear pawed at the beach as he shifted from one front foot to another, his four-inch-long, whitened front claws throwing sand, his back feet stationary. He looked like he was trying to decide whether to bother finishing them off or not.

"Where are you, John?" Bill said, not taking his eyes off the bear.

"We're clear, boss," he answered.

That's all Bill wanted to hear. Bounding over the driftwood, he scrambled back up the bluff. When he looked back, The Warden was ambling back to the whale.

John had gotten Marilyn back to camp by the time Malcolm and Bill joined them.

"Sorry, boss," he said. "She asked me to get her camera bag."

"Pack up," Bill told him. "We're leaving."

For once Marilyn didn't have anything to say.

7

By the time he'd gotten them all ferried back to the lodge, Bill had cooled off a little—but not much. His stomach was still churning; Marilyn had almost gotten them all killed, and a bear mauling wasn't a pretty sight. Bill knew—he'd seen one.

It had happened on the south end of Kodiak Island. Bill had been flying in the area and picked up a distress call on his radio from a helicopter pilot.

"Mayday! Mayday! This is Chopper 45 Kilo over Karluk Lake. Anybody listening? I need help!"

Bill was only ten miles away. "Chopper 45 Kilo, this is Cessna 27 Alpha over Larsen Bay. What's wrong?"

"27 Alpha from 45 Kilo." The response was calmer—

he knew he wasn't alone. "I've got two casualties aboard from a bear mauling and they're both in bad shape."

"Can you make the strip at Larsen Bay?" Bill asked.

"Yeah, I think so, if I don't get sick. The woman's eye is hanging out of her skull on a string."

Bill was only two minutes out; the chopper landed next to his Cessna ten minutes later. While waiting for the rotor blades to stop turning, Bill studied the pilot's face—its color matched the color of the white scarf he was wearing. The name Jack was embroidered on the left breast of his orange flight suit.

When the rotor stopped, Bill ran to the passenger door on the right side of the helicopter and jerked it open. Two bodies—a man and a woman—were lying on the metal floor where the two rear seats should have been.

Bill checked for a pulse on the man, slipping his hand under his bearded chin to find the artery—weak but steady. His right arm jutted out at a strange angle; the elbow of his jacket was sopping wet with blood.

The man's eyes opened when Bill pulled his hand away. "Name's Wilson," he said, in a weak but steady voice. "Becky's worse; take care of her first."

"Got to move you out so we can reach her," Bill said, as the chopper pilot appeared at his elbow. Together, they lifted Wilson out of the aircraft, trying hard not to jostle him too much. Groans, not screams told them they'd done the best they could. They laid him on a blanket on the gravel runway alongside the chopper.

"What about her?" Jack asked, cautiously stepping back from the plane.

Bill jumped into the chopper, crawled across the bloody floor, and felt for a pulse on the woman—very faint but discernible. He rolled her head toward him and her left eyeball flipped over her bloodied cheek, still attached to the optic nerve. The shredded remains of her left ear oozed blood and a slow, pulsing, dark-red stream was coming out of her neck just below the ear. She'd also been partly scalped; the hair on the left side of her head was almost all gone and the skull was oozing blood. It was a wonder the bear's teeth hadn't bitten completely through the skull into her brain.

"Get in here and help me!" Bill shouted. "She's still alive!"

Jack climbed in alongside him. "I'll take her feet," he said. Cautiously, they lifted the unconscious woman from the helicopter and laid her down next to her partner.

Bill had already pulled the first-aid kit from his own airplane. Holding a gauze pad against her neck, he waited until the blood stopped seeping from around his fingers and started to congeal. Her pulse was still there.

"You did a good thing, Jack," Bill said. "If you'd flown straight to town she'd have bled to death in the air. This way she has a chance."

"There's one more back there," Jack said, pointing toward Karluk Lake. "I brought Wilson and Becky out, but I've got to go back and get Larry."

"First, help me load these two in the Cessna," Bill said. Taking a clean gauze pad, he gently moved the eyeball back over its socket and loosely tied a bandage around her whole head. He hoped it would hold. "I'll fly them to Kodiak myself and meet you back here in two hours. We've got to get Becky to a hospital—fast!"

As it turned out, they were a party of surveyors who'd been dropped off in the hills that morning; Jack had been chartered to pick them up at 5:00 that afternoon in a meadow near the outlet of O'Malley Creek, the short stream that drains O'Malley Lake into Karluk Lake. They'd been late arriving at the pick-up point and the pilot had circled looking for them for 10 minutes before setting down.

The three surveyors had been hurrying down a narrow bear trail leading from the ridgeline to the valley. Rounding an alder patch, Wilson had suddenly found himself face to face with a sow and two cubs who were fleeing up the same trail to escape the noise of the circling helicopter.

The cubs scampered into the brush; the sow swatted Wilson to the ground and grabbed his arm with her jaws, breaking it like a twig. It all happened so fast Wilson didn't even have a chance to call out before Becky rounded the corner after him. Seeing the bear, she screamed and started to run back up the trail.

The sow immediately dropped Wilson, rushed after Becky, and knocked her to the ground. Then it grabbed the woman by the head, its powerful jaws crunching down on her skull, and shook the 120 pound woman as if she were a dust mop.

Hearing Becky scream, Larry had his shotgun ready as he rounded the bend. Firing at point blank range, he emptied the slug-loaded, five-shot, semiautomatic riot gun into the bear as it charged.

The sow died at his feet.

Bill got them to the hospital in time to save both their lives—and Becky's eye, which the doctor just popped back into its socket like a grape—but it wasn't something he'd care to go through again.

• • •

Malcolm came out on the dock looking for Bill after supper. Bill hadn't eaten with them; he'd gone to the hangar instead to work off some of his anger, and started changing the landing gear configuration of Charlie's Beaver from wheels back to floats. After an hour, although only partially done with the job, he'd cooled off enough to go out on the dock to watch another spectacular sunset.

Poised over Slope Peak, the sun was ten degrees above the horizon, its slanting rays a brilliant red-orange as they pierced the thin layers of lenticular clouds that hung suspended in the sky to the northwest.

The bay behind the lodge was flat calm; the afternoon

breeze had whispered away to nothing. A dozen Arctic terns who nested on Dog Island a quarter mile away hovered 50 feet over the lake, plunging into the black water to catch small fish, mostly sockeye salmon fry swimming just under the surface. Farther out over the bay, a pair of tundra swans, their huge white wings tinged with orange from the setting sun, flew slowly westward toward their own nesting pond snuggled somewhere on the tundra.

"Marilyn didn't mean any harm," Malcolm said, taking a pipe and tobacco pouch from his jacket pocket.

Bill didn't even turn around. "If The Warden had finished his charge, we'd be just as dead."

"You'd have had to shoot him, I guess." Malcolm began cramming strands of tobacco into the bowl of his pipe. He was either ignoring or didn't even recognize how irritated Bill was. "It's a waste, a magnificent animal like that. But you'd have been justified."

The damn fool was just as bad as his damn fool wife. "Sure I could have shot him," Bill told him. "But that doesn't mean I'd have stopped him. That was no 600-pound sow—that was a 1200-pound boar! There aren't many one-shot kills on any grizzly, particularly when it's charging. At that distance, he'd have been on us before I could reload and fire a second time. And it doesn't take long for a grizzly that size to kill whatever's standing in its way shooting at it—or anybody else stupid enough to be that close."

That was a pretty long speech for Bill. He waited as Malcolm lit a match with his thumbnail and sucked the flame down into the bowl of his pipe. "I don't think Marilyn realized that," he said at last. "I didn't."

The poor guy was trying to make amends, Bill could see that, but what could he do tied to a disaster like Marilyn? "I'm sorry, Malcolm," Bill decided to level with him, "but that wife of yours is a loose cannon around here, and I don't trust her. She doesn't have any common sense, and I'm not risking my neck for her again. Or John's. Or yours, for that matter. This isn't Boston—out here there's no time for arguments. When I tell you to do something, you'd better do it—and fast."

Malcolm took another deep draw on the pipe. "Marilyn doesn't like being told what to do," he admitted. "Got thrown out of college for it."

"This country is a hell of a lot rougher than college," Bill said. "The people who adapt, survive; the ones who don't, don't."

"Marilyn's no coward," Malcolm said, defensively, gazing out at the placid bay, dark brows furrowed, black pupils reflecting the sun. "She was raised rough herself—her father beat her every chance he got. She always fought back. That's how she survived, I guess. Now she thinks she has to."

Bill continued looking out over the bay. He didn't try to stop him from talking.

"She's been reading a lot of first-person stories about famous photographers. You know, those guys who stand in front of a charging elephant or rhino and take pictures. Somehow, she's got it into her head that the way to get the best pictures of dangerous animals is to take chances, like those other guys did. That's why she's a, what did you call her, a loose cannon?"

"Malcolm," Bill said, his patience dwindling, "there are thousands of women in Alaska who didn't have it very easy either. They grew up in a native village on Kodiak Island or a mining town in the mountains or a homestead in the interior—somewhere where there were few people and fewer amenities. Hundreds of these people were teenagers before their families even had running water inside their houses. They lived on what they could catch or raise themselves. They netted salmon in the rivers, dried and smoked it for the winter, grew potatoes and turnips in their gardens. They picked berries, hunted deer or moose or caribou for food, whatever necessary to survive—and they saw a lot of bears while doing it. Grizzly bears."

The sun had crept lower as they talked; it hung a single crimson disc above the hills, its rays slanting upward now to turn the bottoms of the clouds crimson and gold. It would be gone in a minute; already Bill could feel the evening chill through his shirt.

"But," Bill continued, "they all had at least one thing in common. They could recognize danger when they saw it." He turned to walk back toward the lodge.

Malcolm fell in by his side. "Any chance we can go back to the whale tomorrow?" he asked.

"You, yes—your wife, no."

"I can't go without her. We're a team."

"Malcolm, I admire your loyalty but not your good sense," Bill said, angled toward the hangar to shut the door for the night, then continued toward the lodge.

Malcolm was silent until they reached the stairs to the front porch. "I guess we'll leave tomorrow," he finally said, drawing at the last embers in his pipe. "We can come back for the salmon runs later in the season."

Bill shrugged. He could try. It would be Janet's call—and Janet was nobody's fool, not when it came to bears. Especially when she heard how close her only son had come to getting mauled.

8

Gus and Mary Bascomb started on a long-deserved vacation the summer that Bill left for boot camp. They shipped their car to Homer on the Alaska ferry *S.S. Tustamena*, then headed toward Anchorage up the Sterling Highway. Fifteen miles north of Soldotna a drunk driver crossed over into their lane at a speed estimated at 70 mph. There were no survivors in either vehicle.

Bill and Janet both came back to Kodiak for the memorial service and to bury their parents' ashes, then Charlie and I helped them close up their parents' house. There wasn't much; they hadn't accumulated a lot of things, so we stored most of the furniture and Janet took the personal items back to Iliamna with her. The whole thing only took a few days, and both Janet and Bill were still terribly shaken when they parted at the airport.

Years later, when Bill finally opened up and talked to me about it, he said it was the toughest time he'd ever been through, and continued to have nightmares about it for years. He also said it took him three years in the Navy to realize that he still wanted to return to Kodiak again.

Bill went straight to Seattle when his Naval enlistment expired, took a room in a boarding house next to Boeing Field, and, using the financing available to ex-servicemen through the G.I. Bill, began working on his advanced flight ratings with a reputable flight school. When he finally got back to Kodiak six months later, he had a brand new commercial pilot's license with an instrument rating, and a grand total of almost 400 hours in the air.

They didn't laugh outright when he applied for a flying position at Kodiak Airways, but the owner let him know that Bill would need another thousand hours of Alaskan experience before they could even consider hiring him.

Bill might have been discouraged, but didn't show it during the week he stayed with me. We hunted and fished together, then he was off again, this time to Bethel, Alaska. After several dozen telephone calls, he'd finally found an air taxi that was desperate enough to hire a young, inexperienced pilot in the middle of the summer season.

"Did you ask them what happened to their last pilot?" I asked him. The weather for the last three weeks had been miserable around the Island: rain, wind, drizzle and fog. According to the weather reports, it had been that way over most of western Alaska.

"Yeah, and they told me," Bill said, repacking his bag for the next flight to Anchorage. "He got a little careless, flew into some marginal conditions, and dumped a Cessna 207 short of the runway at Aniak. Nobody was hurt but he totaled the plane. They fired him."

"Just you be careful out there," I cautioned him. "They

don't call that area the armpit of Alaska for nothing. The flying conditions are as bad as they are around here, and the living conditions are even worse. That's why they can't get many experienced pilots to work there."

"I know, but I need the job." He left on the morning flight.

• • •

As soon as they'd gotten rid of the photographers, Bill told John to pack a bag, they were flying to Anchorage. He had a few things to say to Janet—and Charlie, too, if he was up to it.

The route to the city was clear and smooth; they cruised through Lake Clark Pass at 2500 feet, counting five moose in the meadows along the river and two dozen white Dall sheep on the steep hillsides. They also saw one grizzly and two black bears along the ridges.

Bill tied down the plane in the transit area next to the fuel pump along the northwestern shore of Lake Hood. As Janet strode purposefully down the ramp to greet them, the first thing he noticed was how much she'd aged. Tall, always slender, now she looked almost angular, her gray hair skinned back into a tight bun behind her ears.

"How's Dad?" John gave his mother a peck on the cheek.

"He's going to live," Janet said, a radiant smile lighting up her face. It was the first time she'd been able to say that in a while. "And he's getting stronger every day. They're flying him to Seattle tomorrow for the operation."

"Let's get to the hospital," Bill said. "I want to see this for myself."

"Thanks, little brother." Janet stopped him, put her arms around his neck, and gave him a big hug. "For everything."

"Forty-seven years old and I'm still a little brother?" Bill tried to back away and look at her, but she grabbed his arm and held on. When he looked down, her eyes glistened. Silently, he stood there and waited until he felt her loosen her grip on the arm, then John took her other arm and they marched silently to the parking lot, Janet setting the pace as she composed herself.

Half-an-hour later they walked into the hospital, a large concrete, brick and steel building on the east side of the city. The fourth-floor nurse, with a telephone in one hand and a patient's chart in the other, recognized Janet and smiled broadly as they passed her station on the way to Charlie's room.

Charlie was in a semiprivate room; the other bed was unoccupied at the moment. Two straight-backed chairs faced the window across the bed; Charlie had shoved his eating tray to one side with the remains of a sickly-looking lunch still on it. When they walked in he was napping. The television, which was mounted on a high stand on the opposite wall, was blaring one of those daytime game shows designed to pass time when you can't think of anything else to do. The poor guy was bored out of his mind.

"You've got company, honey." Janet picked up one of his hands; it looked like it had shrunk a couple of sizes. Before the heart attack he'd been a robust and cheerful man; now his ashen face against the pillow sent a shiver down Bill's spine, and he wondered how long he'd last if they removed all the tubes and needles they had stuck into him.

"Hey there, son," Charlie said, clicking off the TV and smiling at John. "Everything okay down on the homestead?"

"Right as rain," John said. "And just as cheerful without you and Mom."

"Don't worry, we'll be back soon, won't we, Janet?"

"I wasn't so sure a few days ago, hon, but you're looking much better now," she said. "Tell him how good he looks, John."

"More like warmed-up chicken broth," John said, smiling.

"You know your mother," Charlie chuckled. "The eternal optimist." He reached over and squeezed Janet's hand.

Bill never liked hospital rooms—all those suspicious gadgets and tubes hanging around, dials and lights over the bed, the smell of antiseptics, and the ominous bedpan tucked away in a corner. God, how he hated that thing after his own bout with appendicitis a few years ago.

Janet had brightened the room with flowers and cards, but it was still a hospital. Bill walked over and took Charlie's hand. "Good to see you, old timer."

"Hi, Bill," Charlie said, and gave him a big smile. "How'd your season go?"

"A little better than yours, buddy," Bill said, glancing around the room. "These accommodations are a little stuffy, aren't they?"

"All I can handle for now," Charlie said. "But fishing season's coming, and I intend to get out of here before that, which reminds me of something. Crank me up, Janet. John, get that map out of the closet."

"Honey, do you think you should?"

"Do as I ask, woman," Charlie ordered, his face flushing with returning energy. He was back in control again, giving orders like a drill sergeant. "Fishing season's almost here. I've got to tell Bill about the places we fish."

"I can do that, Dad," John offered, getting the Kodiak Sectional Map from Charlie's bag as Janet slowly raised the bed so he could sit up. The Kodiak Sectional covered all of Lake Iliamna, Kodiak Island, and everything in between.

"You know how to fish the rivers, John—not how to land a floatplane in them, taxi, and take off again." Beckoning Bill over to the bed, he spent the next 20 minutes describing each location and what conditions to expect with each change of wind and weather. He described where the underwater rocks and stumps were, where the shallow gravel bars were, what tides to watch out for—everything Bill would need to know to land and take off safely. Charlie was more than just a pilot—he was an observant, meticulous, experienced aircraft commander.

"One more thing, Bill," Charlie said, "and you, too, John. Watch out for the bears, especially that walleyed fish-stealer that gave us so much trouble last season."

John and Bill looked at each other. "I can't imagine what he's talking about, can you, John?" Bill said.

"He can't mean that well-behaved chocolate juvenile who took turns with the others feeding on the whale," John answered.

"Whale? What whale?" Janet asked. Then Bill told them about the photographers.

John finished the story. "The last thing they said was they'd see me again during salmon season."

Charlie looked quickly at Janet. "I say cancel the contract."

"It's a lot of money, Charlie," Janet said. "Our expenses here are pretty high." She was more surprised than anything else—Charlie turning down money was a Charlie she'd never seen before.

"Lives are more important than money," he said, looking around the room that had imprisoned him for two weeks. "I think we should call them up and tell that producer what he can do with his contract." Charlie had been doing some heavy thinking while he'd been lying there. "But it's up to you, Janet. You'll have to run things for a while—do what you think is right."

"I'll cancel it, Charlie," Janet agreed.

"Good," he said. "Now crank me back down. Since you've already refused to climb up here with me, I think I'll take a nap."

"You incorrigible good-for-nothing, Charlie!" Janet blushed as she walked over to give him a big kiss. "You take your nap while I drive my brother back to his airplane."

John settled down with a magazine in his dad's room as they left. "Charlie's a fighter, Jan," Bill said, walking through the revolving door. The air outside the hospital smelled good.

"That's what I keep telling myself, Bill," she said. "But it's nice to hear it from someone else."

9

Bill's return flight from Anchorage that evening was smooth and uneventful; the golden logs and bright red roof of Iliamna Lodge glowed in the evening sunlight as he landed on the gravel runway. Charlie and Janet had built it 20 years ago and named it after the 90-mile-long lake at their doorstep.

The lodge was constructed of logs, each averaging two feet in diameter. It was two stories high, 80 feet long and 40 feet wide, and slept 20 guests in ten double rooms. Charlie had left the huge roof beams exposed in the 25-foot-high cathedral ceiling of the main room that served as living room, dining room, and lounge. Each beam had been carefully trimmed and lacquered to match the golden glow of the exterior.

The kitchen was large and designed for efficiency, as were the walk-in freezer and dry-storage room. The basement underneath was dry and warm. "Someday we're going to finish this off," Janet had explained when she first showed off her new home in the bush to her brother. "It'll make a marvelous recreation area for the staff and guests." But they hadn't completed the basement yet; in the Alaskan bush there always seemed to be something else that needed doing first.

Outbuildings included a 60'x60' hangar and an attached work shop, a 20'x30' bunkhouse for the crew, and a smaller generator shack. The lodge and hangar dominated the grounds, 200 feet apart and separated by a 100-foot-wide runway, one end of which led directly to Slopbucket Lake, a small pond used to wet-store floatplanes overnight. The other end of the 1,200' runway stopped at Roadhouse Creek, a small stream that drained the flatlands around the base of Roadhouse Mountain to the north.

The bunkhouse was near the lodge, the generator shack behind the hangar. The fuel storage tanks for oil and gasoline were supported on log cribs 200 feet away from the hangar. A four-foot-high earth berm around the tanks protected the rest of the property from potential fuel fires or spills.

John flew down from Anchorage the next day; together, he and Bill finished installing the floats on the Beaver, launched and test-flew the plane, and moored it in Slopbucket. They finished by sundown, and none too soon. The first fishing guests arrived the next morning, June 8th.

The salmon don't start their spawning migration from the ocean until late in June, so this first party were all trout fishermen. John and Bill had gone over all the places Charlie had marked on the map and picked out the best trout streams for them.

For the next three weeks John and Bill took several groups of fishermen trout fishing, but they didn't see a bear anywhere. They saw their trails along the banks of the streams and some tracks on the sand and gravel bars, but not a single grizzly. "They come down out of the hills looking for salmon," John told one of the guests, a dentist from Ohio. "When they don't find any, they don't stick around."

"They don't like trout?" asked the dentist, who'd just caught a lovely four-pound rainbow.

"Sure they like trout," Bill answered. "They just can't catch them easily, like the salmon."

"I've known a few fishermen like that," the dentist laughed, nudging his buddy Pete, who hadn't caught anything yet. "At least they have the sense to stay home."

Bill was mostly right. There weren't very many trout compared to the hordes of salmon that come in later, and the trout stay in deeper water. But John had lived there longer, and knew of some bears that lived along the rivers for a few weeks before the salmon arrive—just looking, he supposed. Anyway, that's how Charlie's doctor met his first bear.

By mid-June Charlie'd already been to Seattle for his operation and was back at the lodge, with his doctor along as watchdog. As it turned out, Ben Thompson was not only Alaska's pre-eminent heart specialist, he was also an avid fly fisherman and had jumped at the chance to trade a little professional watchdogging for a couple of weeks of the best fishing this side of the Arctic Circle.

According to Bill's observant sister, Ben was also the most eligible bachelor on the staff at Providence Hospital. Tall, blond, and slender, he was a real charmer among the nurses. Not yet 40 years old, he'd been a heart specialist for several years, first as a military doctor stationed at the Elmendorf Air Force Base hospital in Anchorage, now in private practice in the city. He, Charlie, and Janet took the commercial flight from Anchorage together.

Almost 50 people greeted Charlie and Janet when they arrived at the Iliamna airport. John had spread the word; he and Bill were there with the van but they hardly expected all Charlie and Janet's other friends and neighbors from the villages of Iliamna and Newhalen to show up.

Janet and her husband had befriended most of the locals in one way or another: lent them food and money when they were short, fixed their cars and airplanes, donated to the Russian Orthodox Church, supported the local winter carnival by sponsoring a dog team for the races, and many other smaller ways. Men, women, and several children all shook Charlie's hand as he walked from the airplane to the van. He and Janet took time to speak with every one of them.

Charlie had started putting on a little weight; his face was still pale but his eyes sparkled and his grip was firm as he and Bill shook hands. Janet was sparkling, too, and gave her brother a hug before settling Charlie in the right front seat. She took the wheel herself and they chatted happily as she drove to the lodge.

Things changed pretty fast after Janet and Charlie returned. Charlie couldn't do much but sit around and grumble, but Janet was a human dynamo. Bill hadn't paid much attention to the staff while he'd been there; he seldom even went into the kitchen except to grab a cup of coffee in the morning. The food seemed okay and the service, too; of course, he didn't have much to compare it with—but Janet did.

Two hours after they'd arrived, Mel climbed up on a ladder and started scrubbing the ceiling in the kitchen while his wife started on the shelves in the storeroom. They scrubbed six hours a day for a week, and the two housekeepers were doing the same. "This lodge is going to be full next week and there'll be no time then for spring housecleaning," Janet announced. "We'll do it right and we'll do it now!"

Bill and John were just in the way; the next day they took the doctor trout fishing on Dream Creek, leaving poor Charlie sitting in the lounge when they left. "I'm not much of a trout fisherman anyway, so have your fun," he said, as they waved good-bye. "But you'd better stand out of the way when the salmon arrive." John nodded, knowingly.

Nobody can remember how Dream Creek got its name. It's a small stream that starts in the mountains along the west side of Kamishak Bay. In the spring there's plenty of water from melting snow but by mid-June the water starts to drop, exposing long stretches of gravel beaches on both banks of the creek.

Beavers have lived there for centuries, building houses and dams in several backwaters and side channels. An occasional moose wanders through, nibbling on the tender willow buds along the creek. Several red foxes live in the valley, mink and weasels as well, and an occasional old wolverine, his den up in the foothills, wanders through on his daily rounds searching for food.

Dream Creek flows into the eastern end of Gibraltar Lake, Gibraltar Lake empties into the Gibraltar River, the Gibraltar River runs into Lake Iliamna which, in turn, drains into Bristol Bay, the easternmost arm of the Bering Sea. Although the headwaters of Dream Creek are only a few miles from Kamishak Bay as the crow flies (or the bears walk), the water actually travels west more than a hundred miles before it reaches the sea.

Like most of the Lake Iliamna tributaries, Dream Creek is a spawning stream for both rainbow trout and sockeye salmon, the rainbows in May, the sockeyes in August and September right after the rainbow eggs hatch. Most of the spawning is done in the last two miles of the creek, a winding stretch of stream about 60 feet wide that averages only two to three feet deep. The bottom is sand and gravel and the water flows at two to three miles an hour, both ideal conditions for spawning. Bill circled the stream, flew back to Gibraltar Lake, reduced power, and landed into the ten knot breeze rippling the surface of the lake.

There was nobody else there when they taxied across the lake to the mouth of Dream Creek. As soon as they'd tied the floatplane to some alders near the beach, John led the way upstream along a deeply-trodden bear trail on the left bank. The path was two feet wide and depressed a few inches deeper than the surrounding ground. The heavily compacted earth in the path was almost as firm as concrete; the bears had used the trail for centuries.

John stopped on a wide gravel bar along the creek; he and Ben put their three-sectioned flyrods together, mounted their reels, and strung the lines through the guides. John helped Ben select a fly from Ben's box, picked one out for himself from his own collection, and each tied their flies to the thin monofilament leaders at the end of their lines.

Approaching the river together, John pointed to several trout he could see—dark, two-foot-long, torpedolike shapes finning slowly to hold themselves in the slow current. When Ben spotted the well-camouflaged fish himself, John stood back and let the doctor make the first few casts. A sleek three-pound rainbow streaked off the bottom, gobbled up Ben's fly, and tore off downstream, leaping and slashing to throw the hook as Ben howled in delight. John smiled and walked back to where Bill was standing. He'd done his job.

"You going to fish, John?" Bill asked.

"I'll help Ben land that one, then I might try it myself," he said. "I'm in no hurry. Got all day, got all season for that matter."

Five minutes later Ben eased the tired trout out of the water onto the gravel bar. John knelt down, removed the hook, and slid the fish back into the water. When he stood up, he shook Ben's hand. "Catch a five-pounder and we'll take your picture, Doc," he said.

Ben shrugged out of his day pack, a medium-sized, soft-sided, blue nylon bag, and dropped it on the beach. "Too hot for that thing today."

"Better keep an eye on it," Bill said, walking down to the water's edge.

"Who's going to steal a pack out here?" he laughed. "A bear?" He looked south toward the snow-capped mountains, then turned toward the grassy ridges to the north, looking into the patches of alders and willows upstream for a bear. A tree sparrow flitted past carrying a twig for its nest in the brush, a brace of mallards settled onto a pool upstream, and they could see a bald eagle silhouetted against the blue sky a thousand feet over their heads. With a trout stream full of hungry fish at his feet, Ben was in paradise. He left his pack where it lay.

By lunchtime, they'd moved upstream around several bends and out of sight of the airplane. Alder and willow trees that grew haphazardly along the outside of each turn had impeded their progress, so they'd crossed the creek several times to walk on the exposed gravel bars on the inside of each turn. Bill had already brewed one pot of coffee on the streambank, but they hadn't brought lunch with them.

John saw the bear first. They were on their way back to the beach for the sandwiches they'd left in the plane. Rounding the last bend, they saw a bear sniffing Ben's day pack only a hundred yards away.

"Hey, he's got my pack!" Ben shouted.

Walleye turned and looked straight at them. With Ben's pack under one foot, the bear lowered his head, bit into one corner, and tore it open like a paper bag.

"Damn," Ben said, watching Walleye paw through his stuff: a camera came flying out, his binoculars dropped to the ground, sweater and spare socks flew into the water. Walleye stopped to eat the apple and two candy bars, wrappers and all. "That pack cost me $100."

Walleye tasted the camera, case and all, and they heard the case shatter in his teeth.

"How much did the camera cost, Doc?" Bill asked.

"Damn!"

When they got back to the lodge that night and John told Charlie what had happened, he said, "Time for the bear lecture, I guess."

Charlie took the overstuffed recliner in the lounge, the large blue one with a handle that raised the foot rest that Janet had just bought for him. Janet, John, and Bill, plus Ben and three other guests who had arrived that afternoon, gathered around on the three sofas. They each had a fresh cup of coffee; light from the slowly setting sun to the northwest filled the room, highlighting the steam from their cups.

"There are three times when you have to really watch yourselves around bears," Charlie said, leaning back in his recliner. "Number one, never get between a sow and her cubs. That's simple enough to understand. Number two, stay out of the way of a bear feeding on a moose or caribou carcass, or even a dead seal near the ocean. The only thing that can take a bear's dinner away from it is a bigger bear. Number three, and this is the most important, watch out for a bear with a toothache."

"A toothache!" Ben laughed. "How the hell can you tell when a bear has a toothache?"

"You can't," Charlie said, and put down his cup. Then he sat forward and looked around, pausing to seek the eyes of each guest. "That's why I treat them all alike—with a great deal of respect."

Charlie adjusted his chair to a more comfortable position. "I've had my little joke," and he winked at Janet, "but now let's get serious. You're apt to see bears anytime around here, so you have to know what to do. Suppose you're standing there in the middle of the stream and you've just hooked the biggest fish you've ever seen and a bear comes ambling along, what do you do? Do you land your fish and hope that the bear acts like those nice cultivated bears down there in the lower 48?" Charlie paused to sip the herbal tea Ben had prescribed for him in place of the coffee he normally drank.

"I'll tell you what you do." Charlie put down the cup, looked at Janet, and made a face. He didn't like tea, especially not with bear talk. "You break that fish off, snap the line, and kiss it good-bye—unless you want to fight the bear for it. The same goes for anything else a bear finds, like Ben's pack.

"You can stay out of trouble if you follow a few basic rules," and now Charlie slowed down to emphasize the words, "don't ever run away from a bear—don't even try. I've clocked them running 35 miles an hour in front of my truck between here and the airport. If you have to move out of their way, back off slow and easy.

"Don't scream. Don't shout. Talk to them like you would a friend, quietly. They can hear very well, you know. They won't know what you're saying but they'll understand how you're saying it, and the last thing you want to do is get them excited. And, for God's sake, don't ever, ever, land a fish on the beach in front of a bear."

"Charlie," Ben interrupted. "Why'd that bear attack my pack?"

"Natural curiosity. Besides, it had food in it. A bear has a super-sensitive nose, at least 400 times better than ours. Remember, bears have just six months a year to eat. They take it seriously."

Charlie had that right, too.

10

When someone asks "How long have you lived here?" Alaskans only count the number of winters. Summers are too pleasant to record; when you spend a few winters surviving in the bush, like Charlie and Janet did in Iliamna for so many years, and Bill did in Bethel for three, that's what makes an Alaskan.

Bill returned to Kodiak with over 4,000 hours of flight experience, most of it earned in the uncompromising climate of the western interior. On schedule, rain or shine, he had to fly from Bethel to all the villages in the Yukon-Kuskokwim delta. After the first month of steady flying, he could land the company Cessna 206's and 207's on the short and narrow, gravel strips with hardly a bounce, unload 1,000 pounds of groceries and the mail, load a team of dogs, driver and sled, and the mail, fly to the next village, unload the team, load six passengers and an outboard motor and more mail, and return to Bethel. Then he'd do it again in the afternoon, different villages and cargoes perhaps, but always the mail. In the summers he flew 12 to 15 hours a day, in the short daylight of winter months, six hours from dawn to dark.

And Bill never wrinkled an aircraft; with a resumé like that, Kodiak Airways immediately hired him to fly their Goose, the same plane that Charlie had flown ten years earlier.

When Bill moved back to Kodiak, he bought a piece of land at the end of my street and started to build his own house, a four-room log cabin with a wide front porch and a combination garage/shop attached to the rear. He stayed in my spare room for a few months until he got the roof on, then moved in and finished it at his own pace. I'll have to admit I was a bit surprised when he said he wouldn't need a bank loan; he'd saved almost his entire salary from the Bethel job. Then he said he'd slept in the hangar and ate frozen pizzas most of the time. "Not much to really spend it on out there," was his overall observation of Bethel, "unless you drank a lot." He didn't.

Bill didn't gain his appreciation for hard work from strangers; Gus and Mary were the same way. For that matter, Janet was no slouch when it came to hard work either. I recall when she applied for her first job.

Old Otto Granger told me about it. He was the day foreman at the B and B Fisheries plant on Front Street, one of the larger canneries along cannery row (there were over a dozen canneries operating at the time, processing salmon and halibut in the summer, King crab in the fall, Tanner crab in the winter, and herring, for the roe prized by the Japanese, in the spring). Janet was only 15 but needed some money for Christmas; Gus suggested she try and find some work at a cannery. She started at B and B.

"I told her that we didn't have anything," Otto said, "but that she might try again. Then, I guess, she went home and told her folks what I'd said, because she showed up again the next day after school and asked if I had any work, and I said no, and she came back the next day, and I had to say no, and the next, and then on Saturday morning, and again on Monday afternoon, and by the following Friday I finally smartened up and realized she was going to bug me about work until I gave her some. I told her she could come in every afternoon for two hours and sweep up after the day shift. The place never looked so good, before or since!"

And Otto had been there for over twenty years himself. I guess he ought to know.

• • •

The next day, Ben wanted to go back to Dream Creek.

"I'm not sure that's such a good idea, Charlie," Bill said, slowly shaking his head. "Maybe we ought to let that bear alone for a few days."

"The guy saved my life, Bill," Charlie said, shrugging off his doubts. "Take him anywhere he wants to go."

Bill moored the plane near the mouth of the creek. Later in the morning, while Ben was fishing a quarter-mile upstream, Bill lit a fire on the beach and put on a pot of coffee. When the coffee started boiling he pulled it out of the hot part of the fire and set it on some rocks to simmer while he walked upstream to find Ben.

The fisherman was four bends upriver, standing on a shallow gravel bar about 50 feet from shore. He was casting across to a trout he could see rising to slurp some insects off the surface of the water every few seconds. Bill stopped to watch as Ben expertly whipped his line back and forth a dozen times to dry his fly, 50 feet of fly line whirling back and forth over the stream in tight loops. When he finally dropped the dry fly gently on the surface only two feet upstream of the rising fish, the four-pound trout responded instantly, slashing at the imitation bug with a shower of spray as its head and back came clear of the water. Ben instantly raised his arm over his head, the thin graphite rod arcing in a 90-degree bend.

When the fish felt the hook, it jumped two feet in the air, splashed noisily back underwater, then raced 50 feet upstream, jumped again, dashed back and jumped a third time, all in a few seconds. Ben played the trout deftly, with a wide, boyish grin on his face, and landed it five minutes later on the gravel at his feet. But when he knelt down to unhook and release the gasping fish, a bear woofed from the streambank behind him.

Ben looked up—a bear was standing 50 feet behind him in the alders watching the fish splash frantically in the shallow water. When it stepped out of the alders onto the gravel bar, Bill recognized Walleye.

Then Ben started talking, just like Charlie had told him the night before.

"Hello, Mr. Bear." Ben was still on his knees trying to unhook the fish. Walleye woofed again and stepped a few strides closer—now the bear was only 40 feet away. "Whoa, Mr. Bear, whoa." Snapping the leader, Ben left the fly in the fish's mouth. He slowly stood up and started walking backward across the creek, leaving the hapless trout lying on its side in an inch of water on the gravel bar. While he backed up, he kept watching Walleye and saying, "Whoa there, bear, whoa there, bear, you gotta whoa there, Mr. Bear."

As Ben backed up, Walleye advanced, reaching the trout just as Ben made it over to Bill's side of the stream.

Crunch! The trout's backbone shattered in the bear's jaws. Grabbing the fish, Walleye trotted off into the alders looking very satisfied with himself.

Ben collapsed on the bank, soaking wet from the waist down; the water where he'd crossed was well above his boots. "B-b-bear," he said. "B-b-big b-bear."

"Yeah, I saw him," Bill said. "Friend of yours, too, from the sound of it."

"Did you see his eyes—those little black eyes—looking right at me? Holy Christ, I've never seen anything like it!"

"And that wasn't even a big one," Bill told him. "Wait till you see The Warden." With that, he led the way back to the beach; Ben needed a cup of coffee—bad.

That night, Ben talked so much and so long about his close call with Walleye that Bill and John thought he'd never run down. He told the whole story several times at happy hour, grabbing each new arrival as they entered the lounge. Then he told everyone again at dinner, barely tasting his food as the rest of them chewed silently. Still wound up as tight as a steel spring, he told it again over coffee, then started back at the beginning after they'd settled into more comfortable chairs in the lounge. Finally Charlie'd heard enough.

"Hey, Doc, give us a break," he said. "Sure it's a big bear, but enough's enough. Besides, weren't you going to check me over tonight?"

"Sorry, Charlie, I didn't mean to talk so much, but it was those eyes, those little black eyes, looking right through me..."

"Whoa, whoa, slow down there, Doc." Charlie raised his hand to ward off another recounting, and Ben recognized the signal. He quickly left the lounge, returned shortly with his medical bag, and got down to business, first checking Charlie's pulse and blood pressure, then changing the dressing on his chest. The incision was healing nicely and Ben declared Charlie fit for light duty.

"What's light duty, doctor?" Janet wanted to know.

"Can I go fishing?" Charlie asked, buttoning his shirt.

Charlie loved to fish. Bill and Janet and John all knew that's why he started the lodge in the first place, so he could get to fish all summer long, as often and as long as he wanted to. And he knew the salmon were already on their way to the spawning streams.

"I don't know," Ben shook his head sadly. "Yesterday I would have said yes, no problem, best thing for you. But today I just don't know."

Charlie looked at his doctor silently, a pained expression on his face. Then he looked at Janet and John and Bill, then back at Ben. Then Charlie smiled.

"The hell you say," Charlie had almost believed Ben was serious. "No damn bear's going to keep me from fishing! Tomorrow we go to the Kamishak."

11

The Kamishak River was Charlie's favorite fishing hole: 30 miles long, 150 feet wide, it had the kind of gravelly bottom that salmon swim thousands of miles to lay their eggs in. The meandering stream twists and turns, the spring floods cutting deeply into the steep banks on the outsides of the turns and depositing wide gravel beaches on the insides.

As they flew upriver, they could see the snowy peak of Mt. Katmai 60 miles to the southwest. Towering 6715 feet above sea level, it's still a dominant peak in the area; before it blew its top in 1912, it stood a few thousand feet higher. That eruption was one of the most severe in recorded history, and the volcano rained ash on the region for weeks, burying the river in six feet of dirty, gray sludge. Today, the only remaining evidence is a twelve-inch, whitish-gray seam of compacted clayey material that can be seen about two feet down on the washed out banks.

Bill banked to the left and followed the river back toward the ocean, dipping low to study the many logs and tree stumps which had washed out of the upper valley during the spring floods and floated downstream. They were grounded around every turn along the lower five miles of river, their bare roots and branches waving in the three-knot current.

When Bill flew over the mouth, Charlie pointed out a wide horseshoe bend just upstream of the outlet to the sea. Bill circled twice looking it over carefully for stumps, then landed upstream, immediately reducing the engine power to idle once they were on the water.

Charlie was sitting in the copilot's seat, Ben and John were in back. "Good," Charlie said, looking down at the water surging past the floats; he could see the dozens of gray-backed silver-sided salmon darting away to escape as they taxied slowly toward the beach. "Nobody else is here and the river is full of fish."

Charlie and Bill simultaneously unbuckled their seatbelts and cracked open the pilot's and copilot's doors. Charlie wasn't the pilot but he still thought like one; he started to climb out on his side of the airplane. Sick or not, old habits were hard to change, and Charlie was going to try to help moor the plane.

"Sit still, Charlie, I got it," Bill said, climbed down onto the float, and jumped into the shallows. The air smelled of saltwater and seaweed and clam shells.

When the floats gently nudged up onto the sandy beach, Ben, John, and Charlie followed Bill ashore; Charlie took a deep breath and slowly exhaled. "God, I never thought I'd see this place again."

The soft thunder of surf came from half-a-mile away;

a gull flew overhead, mewing loudly; a fox barked in the alder patch behind them. Charlie smiled—he was finally home.

A few Humpback (usually called humpies or pinks) salmon, swam slowly downstream past the plane. They had already spawned; once they'd completed their life's work, they were aimlessly swimming around—out of habit, nothing else—with bodies splotched with the white fungus that would shortly kill them. Meanwhile, hundreds of fresh Chum salmon were crowding upstream, more and more entering the river on each high tide. The sleek fish, averaging 12 pounds, hadn't yet developed their spawning colors. Now they had grayish-tan backs, silvery sides, and white bellies. Charlie watched them and licked his lips. "That's what I came for."

About an hour later Charlie and Ben were fishing off the sloping gravel beach, standing knee-deep in the water 25 feet from shore. John and Bill were keeping watch from a beached log a hundred feet away when they saw a grizzly approach from upstream. It was on the other side of the river, walking along the bank close to the water.

"I don't recognize that one, boss," John said, looking puzzled.

"It was probably still with its mother last season," Bill said, watching the juvenile amble along.

The three-year-old bear was tannish-brown, the same as most of the bears along the coast. It might have weighed 350 to 400 pounds but not much more. "Bear coming, Charlie," Bill shouted.

Charlie reeled in his line as he walked back to the beach. "Do we have to quit everytime we see a bear?" Ben asked, following Charlie.

"Depends."

"Depends on what?"

"On who he is, and where he is, and what he's doing," Charlie said. "Right now, it depends on my wanting a cup of coffee."

Charlie'd smelled the smoke from the small campfire John had started on the beach. The water was already boiling in an old blackened coffeepot. John made a cup of caffeine-free instant in a tin mug for Charlie, then added some grounds of regular to the rest of the boiling water. Soon they were all sitting on the log sipping coffee while they watched the juvenile walk by. It was looking at the water for fish. "Name it, Charlie," Bill said.

Charlie took another sip and looked at the young bear. He'd been giving the bears names for almost 20 years—just to tell them apart, he said. He took a deep breath of cool, morning air, then another sip of coffee. "Henrietta," he said at last.

Ben turned to look at Charlie, a puzzled look on his face. "How do you know it's a female?" he asked. For some reason, all bears were males to him.

Charlie chuckled. "Didn't you see her just take a leak?" he said, as observant as ever; John and Bill had also seen the stream of liquid coming straight down from her tail. If it had been a male, the stream would have angled forward from between the hind legs.

Charlie got serious again. "Ben, if that bear was on our side of the river, and we all stood firm, I'm pretty sure we could bluff her into going around us. But Miss Paine we don't challenge." He pointed downstream to the sow and her cubs rounding the bend on their side of the river. They all got up and walked back another hundred feet from the water.

The sow walked slowly toward them along the beach, right next to the water, her head down, hips swaying, each hind foot touching the sand slightly before the front foot on the same side. She was intently watching the surface of the stream in front and to the right of her. Her young cubs trailed closely behind.

"That's one of the bears we saw on the whale beach,"

Bill said.

"Looks pretty fat already," Charlie agreed.

She'd put on at least 50 pounds in a month; even her cubs looked bigger.

"Sedge grass won't do that," John said.

"She's been fishing somewhere else, probably the McNeil rapids," Charlie said. The salmon run had started there three weeks ago.

Miss Paine ignored them and lumbered upstream without stopping. Once again, Ben thought he'd missed something. "Didn't she even see us?" he asked.

"Don't kid yourself," Charlie said. "She just knows we're no threat to either her or her family."

"And how does she know that?"

"Experience, more than anything else, I guess," John answered this time. "She's seen a lot of humans along this beach over the years and, evidently, learned to ignore most of us."

"She's one of the smart ones," Charlie said. "As long as we leave her alone, she leaves us alone." He turned his head to look into the sky to the northwest.

Bill had heard the plane too. "Company coming," he said, pointing toward the small dot of another floatplane; when it circled overhead John and Charlie recognized the paint scheme. "The Sportsman's Lodge," John said.

"Yeah, that's Ike's 206 all right," Charlie said. "He's got a pilot flying for him named Randy something-or-other. They run pretty much the same kind of operation we do."

"But we do it better," John said.

The Cessna 206 circled a second time, landed on the same stretch of river, and beached a few hundred yards downstream of Charlie's Beaver. Five people got out and stretched. All but one were dressed in hip boots and yellow slickers. Two of the men walked back into the bushes, reappearing a minute later.

"Too much coffee at breakfast," Charlie observed.

"That Randy?" Bill asked. They were a hundred yards downstream.

"Yeah. The one in the camouflage jacket," Charlie said. "He's probably the reason why that bear stole your fish yesterday, Ben." Charlie turned and headed upstream, a disgruntled look on his face. Bill and Ben fell in by his side while John put out the fire.

"I caught that stupid pilot feeding Walleye three times last year," Charlie said. "He's taught him to beg."

"What do you mean, taught him?" Ben asked.

"You can teach a dog to fetch a stick, or sit up, or roll over, or any number of oddball things, can't you?" Charlie explained. "And how do you teach it? You reward it. You feed it and tell it what a good dog it is, and after a while the dog catches on and does whatever you want without the reward. Well, a grizzly's a lot smarter than a dog and it doesn't take them long to figure out that humans catch fish too, and when they get fed by one or two humans a few times, they start to expect it from all of us."

"Damn stupid, if you ask me," Bill said.

"Not only stupid!" Charlie exploded, and turned around to look back at Randy a quarter-mile downstream. "Damn dangerous! What happens if the humans don't catch any fish—and the bear's still hungry? Who's gonna feed him then?"

Nobody answered; Charlie's logic made too much sense. After they'd walked around the bend and out of sight of the other group, Charlie waded back into the water and started fishing again. He was using the new graphite spinning rod Janet had given him while he was recuperating in the hospital. Pretty soon he laughed as a large salmon leaped high in the air, shook its head, and threw Charlie's lure right back at him. "Try that again and you're mine, you slimy devil," Charlie called to the fish.

"Having fun yet, Dad?" John called. His father just turned and smiled. He'd put Randy out of his mind.

Four hours later Henrietta reappeared, walking down their side of the river. As soon as Charlie saw her, he started backing out of the water to let her pass but Ben stayed where he was and continued to fish.

"Back up, Ben. Let her pass," Charlie said.

"But I'm right over a fresh school of fish," Ben said, casting again. "Why not make her go around us this time?"

"On the operating table, or in the hospital I'll do whatever you say," Charlie said, "but out here you'd better learn to listen to me, if you know what's good for you. Now get your butt out of the water and back up here with the rest of us."

Bill was a little surprised with Charlie's tone of voice, but not John. He'd heard it before. "Dad doesn't take any crap from anybody out here," he said, as they watched Charlie and Ben walk back up the beach toward them.

After the bear passed, Charlie decided he'd had enough fishing for his first day. Fifteen minutes later they followed Henrietta around the curve in the beach and headed for the Beaver. Charlie was walking very slowly; he didn't want to catch up to the young bear.

Randy and the other party of fishermen were strung out along the beach, knee-deep in the shallows, and all casting toward the opposite shore when Charlie turned the corner. Henrietta stopped on the beach only 100 feet away from Randy, who had turned and watched her approach. The pilot took one salmon off of a stringer of fish he'd tied to his waist and threw it toward the bear. Henrietta grabbed the fish off the gravel and jogged back into the brush.

"That does it," Charlie said, and picked up the pace. He walked toward Randy, who had started fishing again. "Hey, I want to talk to you."

"What do you want, old man?" Randy answered, casting again. He didn't even bother turning around.

"I asked you last year to stop feeding the bears."

The pilot/guide reeled in. He was no more than 25

years old, wearing hip boots and a short, camouflage windbreaker over his chamois cloth shirt. He was four inches shorter than both Bill and Charlie's six feet, his face was freckled, and his reddish-blond hair and beard both needed a trim. He slowly walked ashore and stopped 30 feet away from Charlie. His large belt buckle proudly announced *Bush Pilot*.

"Get out of my face, old man," Randy said. "You don't own this river."

"This is a National Park. It's against both the rules and common sense to feed bears in a National Park," Charlie said, keeping his voice steady although Bill could see his face getting redder by the second. "I'm asking you to use a little common sense out here. If we play by the rules, the bears will leave us all alone."

"You want to quit fishing everytime a damn bear walks by, go ahead," Randy said. "I ain't."

"Listen, you idiot," Charlie raised his voice. "Can't you see what you're doing..." He never finished the sentence; reaching for his chest, he started to fall. Bill got to him first, then Ben and John. They grabbed him under each arm before his legs buckled completely.

"Get him to the plane," Ben ordered, feeling Charlie's pulse.

"Aw, I'm okay," Charlie said. His voice was weak but steady as he struggled to get his legs back under him. Halfway to the plane, Charlie had regained his stability and was walking unassisted.

Ben stayed with Charlie while John and Bill walked ahead to untie the two mooring lines and turn the plane around to head toward the river. "Would it do any good to talk to Ike?" Bill asked.

"Ike's worse than Randy," John said. "He's already had his Alaskan hunting guide's license taken away for game violations. He told me once he had to feed the bears just to keep them away from him—just so that his clients could keep on fishing. Frankly, I think Ike would just as soon shoot all the bears out here and be done with it."

Charlie stopped to catch his breath when he reached the plane and sat down on a float to rest. When he looked back toward Randy, Bill sat down next to him and matched his gaze. The towering mountains stood barren and white in the distance, the fertile valley a verdant green, the blue water matching the cloudless sky above them.

"The best salmon stream in the whole of Alaska and that sonofabitch has to ruin it," Charlie said, shaking his head. He stood up and climbed into the Beaver.

12

As soon as they got back to the lodge, Ben took Charlie's blood pressure—185 over 120—and ordered him back to bed. "We'll have no more excitement out of you, Charlie," he said, and turned to Janet. "Keep him quiet for a few days—tie him up if you have to."

Meanwhile, Bill was on the phone to Katmai National Park headquarters in King Salmon to report Randy. It looked like Charlie was grounded for a while, but there was one thing they could do for him. They could make it tougher for Ike and Randy to fish on Charlie's favorite river.

Chief Ranger George Parks was acting as the Katmai Superintendent; the new Superintendent wasn't expected until early in September. Charlie'd commented once about it; it seemed they changed Superintendents every two years, or just when the man started becoming familiar with the job. Few Superintendents that had held the job in the last 15 years liked spending their winters in King Salmon—none of their wives did—and as soon as they got the job, they started angling for a better one somewhere else. "But it's the government way," Charlie'd said, "and the rest of us have to put up with it. Seems like all they really think about is climbing up the bureaucratic ladder to a higher rung." Charlie wasn't too fond of government people.

Acting Superintendent George Parks listened patiently to Bill's discourse, then started one of his own.

"Do you know how big this park is?" he said, more statement than question. "Do you know how many people we have here? I'm already short three experienced rangers this summer, and all the young, college-student yuppie assistants they sent this spring barely know the difference between a bear and a moose. We're doing the best we can under the circumstances..."

"Hey, George," Bill tried to interrupt, but the senior ranger continued without pausing.

"Besides being shorthanded, we've got more visitors in the park this year than we've ever had, and the bear problems on the Brooks River have already started. There's at least a dozen of 'em feeding along the Brooks every day, stealing fish from the sport fishermen, tearing up back packs, you name it, and I haven't got but one ranger to patrol the whole goddamn river." He paused to take a breath.

"I didn't call to listen to your problems!" Bill shouted into the receiver.

George raised his voice to match Bill. "No, but maybe you'll understand when I say we'll try to send someone over there, if we can spare a man—or a woman."

"Anybody, George," Bill said in a more reasonable

tone. "You've got a problem—correction, we've got a problem—and I'm just trying to let you know about it." Bill hung up a minute later, knowing they were on their own anywhere in the park other than at the ranger's summer headquarters on the Brooks River.

The next day Bill took Ben and John back to the Kamishak River. Ben wanted to take a trophy salmon back to town with him, and Janet had her own request. "Bring some salmon back for tonight's dinner," she called after them as they headed for the plane.

"Okay, Mom," John called back.

"Fresh ones!"

"Okay."

"About a dozen. I want to smoke some, too."

"Okay, okay," John said, looked at Bill, and smiled. "Looks like a tough job today, boss, but somebody's got to do it." John was still smiling and humming to himself as they boarded the airplane.

When Bill circled the river an hour later, he saw several schools of salmon half-a-mile upstream from the river's mouth. He landed in the usual place, tied down the plane, and then they walked upstream; Ben hooked a fish on his second cast. After a 10-minute fight, he slid the silvery-bright, eight-pound female chum salmon up on the shore and called to John. "You want to keep this one?"

John walked over and saw that it still had sea lice on it; it was certainly fresh enough. The lice, a whitish, almost translucent parasite about half-an-inch long, drop off the salmon a few days after they enter fresh water. "She's a keeper," he said. "Probably came in on last night's tide."

"Where do we keep them, John?" Bill asked. There were fish-lockers built into the floats of the airplane, but they were already half-a-mile away and he didn't fancy carrying each fish back to the plane as they were caught. And they could hardly leave them on the beach or the bears would get them.

"We'll put them on a stringer," John decided, pulling a short piece of twine from his pack. He poked one end of the twine down the fish's mouth and out the gills, then slipped it through a small loop on the other end, forming a larger loop that ensnared the fish. Then he tied the loose end to a dead tree that had washed loose from the bank and now lay half-buried in two feet of water in the current. The fish swam upright in the eddy behind the stump.

"That will keep them fresh," John said, admiring his work. "What the bears can't see, they won't bother."

The others could see what he meant. As long as the fish was alive, only its camouflaged grayish-tan back could be seen from the surface, and it blended in with the gravelly river bottom so well that the fish was hard to see. A dead fish would turn over, exposing its silvery side and white belly. They'd strung three salmon that way before Henrietta walked down the beach looking for fish; she passed right by the stump with the stringer tied to it without stopping.

Walleye was another story. It didn't take him long to leave Dream Creek and get over to the salmon streams along the coast. Sure enough, there he was in the middle of the stream, slowly paddling along with the current, his head submerged looking for fish. Every ten seconds he'd raise his head above the surface, snort and blow, then take another breath and duck down again. At times, all they could see was the hump between his front shoulders. He was heading right for the stump.

"Damn," John said.

As Walleye reached the stump, he ducked his head and checked the upstream side, where dead fish would fetch up if they drifted downriver with the current. Finding none, he climbed over the stump.

The silhouette of a large grizzly in the sky five feet over their heads terrified the fish; Bill and John both saw the large swirl and frantic splashing on the surface of the river downstream of the stump. Walleye saw it too and leaped right on top of them. Spray and foam filled the air, smaller branches from the stump broke free and drifted downstream, and the water churned. One by one, the bear caught and killed each tethered salmon with a quick snap of his jaws. Then he broke the stringer and waded ashore with his booty.

Walleye didn't bother to unstring the fish—he simply broke the cord. He laid the first salmon flat on the gravel and clamped one foot unceremoniously down on its head. Then the bear lowered his own head, bit into the salmon behind the gills and, by lifting his head, in one swift motion pulled the whole fillet from the backbone.

"That's really neat," said Ben, the surgeon.

After eating the four-pound fillet, ribs, skin, and all, Walleye flipped the fish over and filleted the other side. The second fillet included the tail; once again he ate it all, then ripped open the stomach cavity, dug out, and ate the two sacks of eggs.

Walleye ate one more fish while the fishermen watched, then picked up the last one and carried it into the brush.

"Damn bears," John said, walking over to pick up the shredded stringer. "I should have known that sonofabitch would be back," and he kicked at the gravel, sending a shower of stones splashing into the water. Then he stood frowning at the place where Walleyed disappeared, slowly shaking his head. He didn't say another word, but Bill and Ben could see his lips moving.

"Let's have lunch," Bill called, and threw more wood on the campfire. John finally turned away and scuffed up the beach, then rummaged through the lunch box and slapped the food onto a blanket. Bill refilled the coffee pot with fresh water from the river, then grabbed a sandwich. They ate in silence.

After lunch, John started stuffing the garbage into a black plastic bag when he suddenly stopped and looked at the river. "Hey," he said, looking at the bag. "Why not put the next fish in a bag and then put the bag in the water? We can weight it down with stones. Even if a bear does see it, he won't know there's a fish in it." John was smiling again.

Ben hooked another salmon right after lunch, and John helped him land it, a heavy male of about 14 pounds with half-a-dozen sea lice clinging to the body near the tail. The fish had started to change color; reddish-purple vertical stripes were now faintly visible along both sides of its body, but the presence of the lice assured them it was fresh. Some of the fish start changing into their spawning colors within hours after entering fresh water.

John never let the fish touch the beach; he cleaned it in the shallow water so that all the smells of fish blood and slime washed away and there was nothing left to attract the bears. After throwing the viscera and head into deep water, he carefully slid the pinkish-orange fleshed fish into the black plastic bag, carried the bag further into the river and buried it beneath several stones in about a foot of water.

By three that afternoon they had four more fish in the bag when Ben hooked his trophy—it looked to be at least 20 pounds when it jumped. Ben shouted with delight; after the fish jumped, it ran 150 yards down the river, thrashed on the surface in a foamy blur, and turned back upriver again. Ben stripped his line in as fast as he could, but the large salmon was too fast and strong—as soon as it got back upstream, it tore off downstream again. Then Walleye returned.

"Hurry up and get that fish in the bag!" Bill shouted. Walleye was sniffing along the shoreline only a hundred yards away.

Just then the salmon streaked across the river in another frantic rush for freedom, leaping clear of the water in a silver arc, splashing back in a shower of spray.

"Slack off, Ben," Bill called, walking down onto the beach with his rifle over his shoulder. "You'll never land that fish before Walleye gets here so let's see if we can bluff him to go around us."

Ben slacked off the tension on his line; as soon as he did that, the salmon quit fighting and held quietly in the current. Walleye continued to amble toward them.

Ben, John, and Bill were standing along the shore only a few feet from the river. "Get out of here, Mr. Bear!" Bill shouted. "We're staying here! You go around!"

The bear stood his ground. "Go on, Mr. Bear," Bill shouted again. He advanced a few steps toward him. "Get out of here!" Bill called again, then picked up a small rock from the beach and tossed it at the bear. It fell harmlessly 15 feet in front of his feet.

Walleye shuffled a little, dancing on his front feet while his back feet remained still. He swung around sideways, then turned back and stood up on his back feet. Now his head was two feet higher than Bill's. Jacking a shell into the chamber of his rifle just in case, Bill threw his arms wide, danced back and forth, and shouted *HAAR-WAAAAA*! at the top of his voice.

Walleye was so astonished he dropped back on all fours and dashed up the beach, disappearing into the brush.

"Okay, Ben, land that fish," Bill said, watching to make sure Walleye didn't come back.

Ben landed his trophy at last, but it was still flopping in the shallows when Miss Paine showed up, trotting along the beach with her cubs running along behind trying to keep up with her.

"John, get that fish in the bag—now!"

John shoved the half-cleaned salmon into the bag and quickly piled the stones on top of it again to keep it underwater. He sprinted back to join them, standing 100 feet away from the river on the gravel bar. Thirty seconds later the sow reached the spot along the shoreline closest to the bag.

Miss Paine paused to look around. She glanced at the cubs briefly, then looked upstream and down, her large head moving slowly and deliberately, taking in everything. Her front feet were barely under water, her hind feet on the dry land. Just as she turned to walk away, the half-dead salmon started thrashing inside the bag and a corner of black plastic broke free and poked up through the surface of the river. The bear saw it, too.

"Damn," John said.

"Double damn," Bill said, as Miss Paine waded toward their cache. Scattering rocks, she ripped open the plastic with one swipe of her paw, exposed the fish, and sat down in the water in front of them. She ate them all. Her cubs got the scraps.

"My nemesis," Ben said, watching his huge salmon get filleted.

"That last one was supper, John," Bill said, looking at his watch. "What are you going to tell your mother?"

"She's heard it all already—from Dad," John said. "He doesn't always bring salmon home either. Guess it's cold beans, cold potato salad, and cold cuts tonight. Let's get out of here."

But when they got back to the lodge, they found Charlie's day had been even worse than theirs. Ben checked his blood pressure again; it was back to normal and the color was back in Charlie's ruddy face, but he wasn't happy.

"Our lawyer called today," Charlie said, glancing at his wife. "If we don't take the photographers back, they're going to sue, and a law suit now will bankrupt us."

"Even if we win," Janet added. "Our expenses this spring almost wiped out our savings anyway. We can't survive a long drawn-out law suit."

"We've got to take them back," Charlie said.

Bill looked at him with amazement. "Marilyn's uncontrollable, Charlie," he warned.

"From what I've heard, you had her under control most of the time."

"I had to pick her up and carry her off the beach—twice,

in two days! What kind of control is that?"

"At least it worked," Charlie said. "Did her husband object?"

"No," Bill answered. He looked out the window at the water, thinking, then turn back to face the group. "Actually, I think he approved. But it's no damn way to operate out in the bush."

"It damn well isn't." Charlie had been giving it some thought. "But we've got to try. We won't let the woman out of our sight, that's all. It'll take at least two of us every day."

"Two of *you* every day," Ben interrupted. "Charlie's not going anywhere for a while."

"Right," Janet agreed, and looked at her husband. "You heard him, Charlie."

"Yeah, okay, okay, I'll stay put for a while," Charlie said. "So it's up to Bill and John. Take turns, watch her like a bear stalks a salmon. Keep her out of trouble."

"When do they get here?" John asked.

"Two days from now."

"Triple damn!"

13

Marilyn opened the lounge door with a swoosh. She stopped just inside the room and glanced quickly around to see that everyone was watching her—and Bill knew it was war. Ignoring him, she walked straight toward Charlie and Janet and started talking to them as if she were an old friend. When she finally looked Bill's way, she smiled one of the craftiest smiles he'd ever seen—all teeth, no humor. She nodded her head, flipped her long blond hair over one shoulder, and turned back to Janet. Total war—nothing less—and she made sure he'd gotten the message.

When Malcolm came into the lounge five minutes later, he met Bill halfway across the room. His own grin was genuine and Bill steered him over to meet Charlie and

Janet, who were still listening to Marilyn describe their journey (tedious), the weather in Anchorage (hot), how well the film from their first trip came out (simply marvelous), and how they looked forward to seeing more bears along the salmon rivers. Bill drew Malcolm aside; he didn't need to hear all that babbling either, and they went out on the porch to watch the sunset.

"I'll be flying you and your wife, you know," Bill said.

"I'm counting on it." Malcolm took out his pipe again and started stuffing tobacco into the bowl.

"What do you mean, you're counting on it?"

"I'm counting on you to keep her out of trouble," Malcolm said, a crafty smile lingering at the corners of his mouth.

"Me? She's your wife!"

"You don't understand." Now Malcolm grinned. "The film we shot on the beach was really good, and the closer we got to the bears, the bigger they looked. The producers were ecstatic, particularly with the pictures she got before you carried her off the whale beach. That footage was really something!"

"I'll bet," Bill said, remembering the machine-gun clicking of The Warden's teeth. Nobody in their right mind forgets that sound.

"So I'm afraid there's no holding her back," Malcolm said. "She won't listen to reason, and the producers are egging her on."

Bill knew he should have walked out right then, jumped in his plane, and headed back toward Kodiak. If it wasn't for Janet and Charlie, he would have. Instead, he got a plate, filled it at the buffet line, and joined the others at dinner. Only Janet smiled at him as he ate in silence at the far end of the table.

The conversation held little interest for Bill until Marilyn asked, "So where are all the bears you promised, Charlie?"

"There are plenty of bears at the Brooks River," he

answered her, stirring his coffee. "That's a real popular spot for photographers."

"And?" What a persistent bitch.

"We've seen a few on Dream Creek."

"And?"

Malcolm interrupted. "On the way in from the airport, John said something about the coastal rivers having a lot of bears."

Charlie hesitated, then agreed. "Yeah, that's another good bet this time of year."

"Which one, Charlie?" Marilyn asked.

Charlie slowly put down his cup and turned to look at her, then he looked at John, who blushed under his glare. Charlie hadn't intended on sending Marilyn to his favorite river but he hadn't told any of them about it, and poor John had inadvertently let the information slip out to her husband. When Charlie finally answered, "The Kamishak River," Bill stood up and left the room. Charlie didn't need to tell him where he'd be flying in the morning.

Fog delayed their departure the next day—even Marilyn had to agree it wouldn't do much good filming in such low visibility. They finally departed the lodge in the early afternoon; Forty minutes later Bill landed in the same stretch of river they'd been using for the past two weeks.

An unusually high tide had been ebbing for about an hour when they arrived. The receding tide had left several large shallow pools on the flat exposed beach. Hundreds of fresh chum salmon had entered the river at high water and about a dozen of them had strayed from the main channel and swum into two of the larger pools. These fish were temporarily cut off from the deeper river water by gravel and sand bars. As Bill and his party waded upstream, the water in the pools came up to their knees in some places, their ankles in others.

"Want to catch some of these fish, boss," John suggested. They could see them slowly finning in the clear shallow water.

"Let the bears have them," Bill said.

"Bears can catch those fish?" Marilyn asked.

"Just watch," John said. They'd already spotted Walleye walking toward the pool. "Back up and give him room."

Trotting up to the edge of the water, Walleye saw one of the fish dart away from under his feet, and the chase was on. The bear charged across the pool, then back; losing contact with the fish, he stopped and stood up on his back legs to get a better view, then dropped back on all four feet and pounced across the pool again. The fish darted ahead, trying to escape in water that was rapidly becoming more and more muddy from sediment churned up under the bear's huge feet.

Malcolm quickly set up his camera and stood photographing the bear from 100 yards away. Marilyn took one look through her lens, then picked up her tripod-mounted camera to start walking toward the tidal pool.

She got halfway to the pool before Bill reached her. Grabbing hold of the back of her fluffy, down-filled jacket, he stopped her in her tracks. "That's close enough."

"Let go of me," she said, trying to jerk free.

"That's close enough, I said."

"The hell it is," she said, slipping her arms out of the jacket.

Bill grabbed her braids. "Film from here or I'll carry you back." His voice was calm but determined.

"Damn you, Bascomb!" she shouted, turning to her husband still filming from a safe distance. "Malcolm, tell this bastard to let me go."

"Cool it, Marilyn," Malcolm said. "If Bill says you're too close, you're too close."

"Damn you both!" Marilyn shouted. "The producers said they wanted close-ups!"

"Use the bigger lens—that's what we brought it for—but get to work." Malcolm wasn't losing his cool. "How long do you think that bear's going to race around in front of us like that?"

The pool was 60 feet long and half as wide. Back and forth the salmon darted, leaving torpedolike wakes in the water's surface that Walleye followed at a full gallop, churning up yet more mud. Finally, one of the fish failed to make the turn at the other end of the pool; it slid part way out of the water on the sand, fell on its side and flopped wildly trying to right itself. The bear pounced with both front feet.

It always seems such a waste when the bears attack healthy salmon. Once the fish have spawned, no one minds when the bears feed on the dead and dying—after all, they've already fulfilled their purpose. But to take the fresh ones before they've laid their eggs and sperm and started a new generation, that seems a loss.

Only half the eggs hatch in the first place, and the long migration to salt water puts the little fry directly in the path of waiting trout and char, who gobble them up by the hundreds. Then the perils of the sea await. Of the 3,000 eggs laid by the average female salmon, only three or four survive the onslaught of the many salt-water predators waiting to attack them for food: seals, sea lions, Belugas and Orcas (killer whales), and the most efficient of all, the commercial fishermen with miles of nets stretched across the salmon's path.

But bears have to eat, too, and they're at the top of their own food chain. They take advantage of anything they can catch; shortly after Walleye'd caught and eaten his first fish, he was joined by Miss Paine and her cubs.

Miss Paine approached the tidal pools from the same direction as Walleye had, but she stayed about 100 feet away from the boar, and skirted around Walleye's pool to get to the unoccupied one. Her fishing technique was identical to Walleye's, and the cubs splashed and ran pell-mell after their mother until she finally trapped a fish. Miss

Paine ate the salmon herself, then left the scraps, backbone, and head for the cubs as she re-entered the pool and chased down another salmon.

Together, Walleye and Miss Paine finally cleaned out all the salmon that had strayed from the main channel into the two tidal pools. When the tide returned, the rising water reconnected the pools to the main river, and the bears moved upstream.

Bill and his party had just started moving upstream to follow when an Arctic tern rose off the beach and started to dive at them, loudly complaining *keer-keer-keer* with every swoop. About the size of a crow, the black-capped, gray-and-white bird is one of the greatest aerialists in the avian family.

"Hold it," Bill said. "There's a chick somewhere along here, and we don't want to step on it."

Soon Marilyn spotted the small fluff of brownish-gray feathers hidden among the stones. Only 20 feet in front of them, the chick was huddled beside a stone of about the same shape and color.

"Look," Marilyn said, inching forward toward the chick as it scampered away toward another rock. "Isn't it cute, Malcolm."

"*Keer-keer-keer*" the adult bird cried, diving again to strike Marilyn's hat with its beak.

"Leave it alone, Marilyn," John said.

Marilyn crouched down to get a little closer. The chick was now only five feet away.

"*Keer-keer.*" The parent dove again, this time driving its bill into Marilyn's hat.

"Ow!" she cried, leaping to her feet and rubbing her head. "That hurt."

"Lucky you were wearing a hat or it would have drawn blood," Bill said. "Now back off!"

"Where's the nest?" she asked.

"They don't make a nest, they lay their eggs right in the

stones," John said, helping her back up the gravelly beach with her equipment. "You're apt to find them anywhere."

They filmed for another few minutes; finally leaving the birds, they walked another 100 yards upstream and came to a large backwater. Dead and dying Humpback salmon littered the beach here; these fish had already spawned upstream on some underwater gravel bar in the river, then swum slowly and aimlessly downstream until they were near death, finally fetching up on the gravel at Bill's feet. The fungus-covered, decaying carcasses were the photographers first look at dead salmon.

"What happened to their eyes?" Marilyn wanted to know, walking up beside him.

"The birds get them," Bill said.

"Don't be ridiculous," she said—apparently she wasn't going to believe anything Bill told her. She walked closer to the water to inspect the rotting fish, covering her nose against the smell, a pungent, nauseous odor of decaying food as strong as any skunk smell.

"Bill's right," John said. "We've even seen gulls peck out the eyes of live fish."

"Sure you have," Marilyn teased him. "I suppose they dive underwater and chase them, too." She turned back to her camera, preparing to photograph the dead humpies when another fish swam slowly toward the beach, fell onto its side in a few inches of water, and began quivering as it lay gasping on the sand. The once-silvery fish's back and sides were almost black, its stomach milky-white, and the head, including the eyes, was half-covered with a whitish fungus.

"Ugh," Marilyn said, focusing her camera on the floundering male fish. "What an ugly thing that is."

"Ugly or not, that's one of the winners," Bill said.

"A winner?" Her voice was all sarcasm.

"You heard me," he said. "In the battle for survival, he beat the odds—a thousand to one—and made it back to spawn. Yes, Marilyn, I'd call it a winner."

Marilyn didn't have an answer, for a change.

"Here comes Walleye again," John called, as the bear trotted up to inspect the eddy. Grabbing the half-dead salmon, he wolfed it down and then began pawing at another one lying there already coated with fungus over its whole body. After one taste, he dropped it and walked away.

"There are some things too rotten even for the bears," John said.

14

"What the hell are you doing here, Bascomb?"

Bill had just entered the lounge and was walking toward the bar to pour his usual scotch and water before dinner. A minute later, with a drink in his hand, he slowly turned around. He'd already recognized Cal Edgecombe's biting growl.

Cal might have added a few more pounds to an already ample gut, and his flushed face still showed the effects of the expensive bourbon he'd been drinking at bear camp (Bill had noticed one of the bottles standing half-filled on Charlie's bar). Otherwise, Cal looked the same: 5'9", 50 years old, with graying reddish-blond hair around the ears but bald on the top. Today he was wearing a white silk shirt open at the neck, dark green woolen trousers, and the usual custom-engraved leather cowboy boots.

"I'll ask you the same question, Cal," Bill answered, taking a good swig of his own drink. They were the only ones in the room.

"I came to fish," Cal said. "I'm surprised you'd show your face anyplace after that ridiculous bear hunt you took me on."

"Janet's my sister," Bill said, ignoring the slur. "I'm flying for Charlie this season."

"If I'd known you were here, I'd sure as hell gone someplace else," Cal said, watching Marilyn walk into the room and cross to the bar. "But, what the hell, one pilot's as good as the next out here. Isn't that right, honey?"

Cal was a pilot himself, and should have known better. Charlie would straighten him out with his 'old, bold pilot' story; there are old pilots and there are bold pilots, but there are no old, bold pilots in Alaska, or anywhere else for that matter. Competent, seasoned pilots—mature men and women with thousands of hours in the air under the severest flight conditions—are hard to find, and any dumbbell who claims that one pilot's as good as the next, especially bush pilots, is showing his own ignorance.

Malcolm followed his wife to the bar to mix them a drink, a beer for Malcolm, spritzer and lime for his wife.

"Hello," Marilyn said, turning to Cal. "We're the Fosters, Marilyn and Malcolm Foster, so nice to meet you Mr.?"

"Edgecombe, ma'am, Cal Edgecombe, and the pleasure's all mine," Cal said, his voice dripping with charm. He looked Marilyn up and down as she crossed the room to shake his hand. He'd turned into a southern gentleman so abruptly, Bill thought for a second he was going to bend down and kiss her hand before Malcolm arrived with the drinks.

"And where have you been all day," Cal asked, shaking

hands with Malcolm.

"Watching bears," Marilyn said. "Lots of bears, and they were catching salmon right in front of us. Oh, it was soooo exciting, Mr. Edgecombe, and we took pictures of them all afternoon."

"Please call me Cal, honey. Now, how many bears did you see?"

"Lots," Marilyn said. "I'll bet we saw at least a dozen or so, wouldn't you agree, Malcolm?"

Cal turned toward Bill. "You didn't show me half that many bears when we were hunting, Bascomb," he called across the room. His combative tone had returned and Marilyn caught the drift. She grinned up at him, encouragingly, as Bill picked up his drink and headed for the kitchen, passing Janet on his way.

"I'll eat with the help tonight, Sis," Bill said. "I've had enough of your guests for one day."

Later that evening, as Charlie was pouring over his area maps, he suggested Bill take all of the guests to the same river, finally settling on the Kamishak again.

"Marilyn's bad enough," Bill protested. "Cal on top of that is too much!"

"Saves on gas," Charlie grunted, always the one to save a buck where he could. "Besides, I can't send John off with Cal—you need him. Maybe Ben can help keep Cal busy."

"At least let Janet come along," Bill argued. Janet liked to fish almost as much as Charlie did. "She hasn't been out of the lodge in weeks."

"Good idea, Bill," Charlie said, turning to his wife. "Want to go fishing tomorrow?"

"Sure, if there's room in the plane," she said, and Bill breathed a little easier. With Janet along to help watch Marilyn, Bill and John would have time to switch back and forth between Marilyn and Cal. Bill didn't expect Ben to help with the others, but he didn't need watching anymore. He'd learned how to keep himself out of trouble.

With this plan in mind, all seven boarded the Beaver shortly after breakfast, Malcolm riding copilot again, with Cal and Marilyn in the center, and Ben, John, and Janet in the rear seats. With no fog to delay their departure, and a bright morning sun to set the lake shimmering, Bill took off into a 10-knot breeze, circled the lodge once for some more pictures Malcolm wanted, then headed toward the Kamishak River.

They had the river to themselves again, but found only a few salmon trapped in the tidal pools. Malcolm suggested they might wait there for the bears again, but Cal refused to wait. "I came here to fish," he said, his fishing rod already assembled. "You want to wait around for a bunch of damn bears, go ahead. I'm going fishing," and he started walking upriver along the wide gravel beach. Bill didn't have much choice but to follow, and the rest of the group fell in step behind him.

They stopped a few hundred yards upstream of the airplane to watch a large salmon leap clear of the water at mid-stream and splash back in. The salmon leaped twice more in as many seconds, and Cal dropped his tackle box on the beach. "I'm fishing here," he declared, and walked down the almost-flat gravel-covered beach toward the river. He waded in until the water was up to his knees, then made his first cast, retrieving the large red and white lure with sharp jerks. Ben and Janet stopped to put their fly rods together and started fishing downstream of Cal. Malcolm and Marilyn lay their camera bags down near the fire pit they'd used the day before and started getting their equipment ready, while John started gathering driftwood. Bill took a seat on a nearby log.

Cal was using a spinning rod, Ben and Janet fly rods; Cal hooked a fish just as Ben and Janet entered the river, and landed his fish in two minutes, dragging it unmercifully up the beach on 30-pound test line while Ben and Janet started casting. Smacking his salmon on the head with a stick, Cal unhooked it and threw it into his ice-packed cooler. Janet hooked her first salmon as Cal slammed the lid back onto his ice chest.

Just then, Miss Paine and her two small cubs walked out of the brush and ambled onto the broad gravel bar a few hundred yards upstream. The sow sniffed along the edge of the river, then started trotting downstream toward them.

"Janet, bear coming," Bill called, pointing to Miss Paine. "Break that fish off. John, help her."

Marilyn rushed up the beach with her camera on her shoulder as Cal started to wade back into the water. "Back up, Cal," Bill barked, and saw him start to object until he looked up and saw the size of Miss Paine. Now over 700 pounds, the sow sure looked like she meant business, with two cubs running to keep up. Cal returned to the gravel bar.

John ran out to help his mother. Grabbing her line, he pointed the rod at the fish and jerked several times, each time harder than the last. The line should have broken, but it didn't.

"Damn," Bill said. Things sure can get out of hand in a hurry. He ran into the water to try and break the line himself. "John, watch Marilyn." Bill jerked his thumb at the woman and John loped up the beach to be sure she stayed away from the bear.

The line wouldn't give. The sow was now only 100 yards away, still trotting toward them, looking at the water for salmon. Still holding Janet's rod, Bill walked back up the gravel bar allowing the slackened line to run freely off the reel. The hooked salmon swam back to mid-stream.

Bill stopped about 60 feet back from the water, Janet, Ben, and Cal backing up to join him. Malcolm had his camera set up to film the human-bear encounter as John herded Marilyn back to join the group.

So far they'd done everything right. Even the salmon stopped thrashing when Bill released the tension on the line. It was now quietly holding its position in the current.

The fly line lay flat along the gravel beach; the bears should walk right over it without paying any attention—then Bill noticed the problem. Directly in the path of the sow was a cobble five to six inches round, and the fly line was right across the top of it, raised a few inches above the other stones. He was holding a perfectly placed trip wire, and the bears were less than 50 feet away.

It was too late to do anything. If Bill tried to lift the line off the stone, the fish might start struggling again, right in front of the hungry sow. Bill quickly put down the rod, picked up his rifle, and loaded a round in the chamber. He wouldn't shoot the sow for stealing the fish, but who knows what other mischief she might get in. The metallic click-click of the bolt made an ominous sound in the still, morning air.

Miss Paine shambled up to the fly line and deftly stepped over it. Then the first cub jumped over it. Bill was about to congratulate himself when the second cub tried to jump over it, too, but the line caught on the hair above the little claws on its left front foot. The cub started dragging a vee in the line as it followed its mother.

"The line's caught, Bill." Janet said.

"I'm not blind."

"What can I do?" John asked.

"Pick up the rod, John, and make sure the reel doesn't hang up," Bill said. "Feed in as much slack as you can."

They were whispering. Although the sow was headed away from them, she was still within earshot. Then the young bear looked down and saw the fluorescent-green fly line across its foot.

The cub jumped, rising on its hind legs, but the line stuck as though it were glued. Then the cub dropped back on all four feet and jumped again—and again, and then again, each jump carrying it backward a few inches. After the sixth jump, the tension on the line slackened enough so that the fly line dropped free, and the cub galloped off to catch up with its mother.

They all stood there silently watching the trio of bears walk around the next bend downstream.

"It never made a sound," John said, after the bears disappeared. "Not a moan or squeal, nothing."

"What would have happened if the cub had squealed?" Ben asked.

"I don't know," Bill said. "If it had pulled on the line much longer, the salmon would have started thrashing again. Either way, the sow would have turned back to investigate."

"Then what?" Marilyn asked.

"Only the sow knows that," Bill said, then opened the bolt on his rifle, removed the cartridge from the chamber, and slid it back into the magazine.

"Would you have shot it?" she asked.

"Not for stealing a fish, I wouldn't, but if she charged back here to protect her cubs, I might have had to shoot."

"The cubs too?"

"No, not the cubs, Marilyn," Bill explained. "But when young cubs are abandoned, for any reason, their chances of survival in the wild are slim. If another sow adopted them within a few days, they might make it—otherwise, they'd be dead meat."

"So you might as well shoot them, then, if you shot their mother," Marilyn said. "Is that what you're saying?"

"Who cares," Cal interrupted. "Let's go fishing." He waded back into the stream, and Bill was just as happy he did. That conversation was getting nowhere.

John handed the fly rod to his mother. "You'd better land that salmon before it gets us into any more trouble."

As soon as Janet tightened her line, the rested salmon streaked across the river again, leaped in a silvery spray near the opposite shore, then raced downstream as if it had never been hooked before. Janet played the fish patiently, reeling in line when she could, giving slack when the fish pulled harder, and finally landed it 10 minutes later.

"I want this one for dinner, John," Janet called, and he ran down to help her unhook and kill the fish.

"This time I'll put it in the floats," Bill said, and handed John a plastic bag. John slid the whole salmon into the bag and handed it back, as his mother started to cast again.

"Wait a sec, Mom," John said. Wading into the stream, he cut the fly off her line, tied on a piece of 10-pound tippet, and retied the fly to the end of it.

"Now the line should break when we want it to," he said.

In two more hours Janet had caught three more fish, Cal four more and Ben half-a-dozen, so Bill decided to stop for a break. Lighting a fire on the beach, he threw some grounds into the bottom of a #10 can and boiled up some fresh coffee.

"There doesn't seem to be many bears around today," Malcolm said, taking his cup and gulping down the hot coffee after lunch. "You suppose I could try my hand at fishing?"

"Sure." John was only too happy to discover a new convert, and rigged his own fly rod for the photographer.

"Hey, how about me?" Marilyn complained. "Don't I get to fish?"

"I've caught a lot of fish this morning," Cal said. "You can use my rod for a while, little lady. Come here and I'll show you how." The two of them walked toward the water, Cal with his arm around Marilyn's shoulders.

They fished that part of the river for another hour as Bill kept watch. The bears were apparently all sleeping or something and stayed away. Things seemed so quiet, Bill decided to walk upstream to look over some of the other fishing holes John had told him about. On his way back, he saw Cassius walking down the other bank.

"Bear coming," Bill called as he returned to the beach. Cal, Janet, Ben, and Malcolm were still fishing. Marilyn had gotten bored and was sitting on the beach, reading a book.

"So what," Cal shouted from the middle of the river as the others started wading back. "I still have another cooler to fill before I go home."

Cassius was a long-legged, mangy-looking boar who weighed almost 800 pounds. His discolored hide was rubbed down to the soft under-fur along his back and hind legs. "Don't be stupid," Bill said. "He'll go away soon enough. Just give him a little time."

"You've got a gun," Cal said. "Shoot the bastard. I want to fish."

Cassius sat down on the far bank directly across from them, then rolled over to rest his head on a clump of grass and closed his eyes.

"Look at that!" Cal yelled. "The damn thing will probably lie there all day!" Then Cal deliberately cast his lure toward the opposite bank right under the bear's nose, and retrieved it slowly. Marilyn ran to get her camera.

A 12-pound fish rose from the bottom of the river and devoured the wobbling spoon on Cal's line. Swiftly raising the rod, Cal set the treble hooks into the salmon's jaw. When he stepped back, the fish leaped straight up into the air with the lure dangling out of its mouth.

Cassius opened his eyes and sat up. Bears see a lot of fish jump in the course of a summer; when a salmon jumps out in the middle of the stream, they seem to know they can't catch it and don't pay much attention. No one will ever know why Cassius stood up just then, maybe it was just time for him to move on.

"Don't land that fish," Bill shouted to Cal. "That bear's too close."

"You handle the bear," Cal said, stubbornly putting his back and arms into the fight. Using a stout rod, with the drag set tightly on the reel, Cal soon had the bright fish flopping wildly in the shallows.

Cassius watched the whole fight; seeing the flash of silver, the bear charged into the river, hitting the water in full stride and swimming toward them with powerful dog-paddle strokes. Once his feet touched the gravel bar, the hungry bear lunged for the fish.

"Drop that rod and get out of there!" Bill shouted at Cal.

"Drop nothing!" Cal started running up the beach dragging the salmon behind him. "That bastard isn't getting my fish!"

"Drop it, you damn fool!" The bear cleared the water and charged up the beach chasing the skidding fish. Bill sighted his loaded rifle on his neck; as much as he disliked Cal at that moment, he couldn't let the bear reach him. Flipping off the safety, Bill started to squeeze the trigger.

Cal hadn't looked back. When he did and saw how close the bear was, he dropped his rod and started to run, but he tripped over his cumbersome fishing boots and sprawled full-length in the sand, gasping and crying for help. Cal was only 30 feet from the salmon. If Cassius didn't stop for the fish, Bill would have to kill him.

Cassius stopped and picked up the salmon—that's all he wanted. With the fish firmly clenched in his jaws, he turned and ran for the alders, dragging the rod and reel behind him. Cal had tightened the drag on the reel so much that the spool was frozen in place and the line couldn't pull free. When Cassius had vanished into the woods, Bill eased the pressure off his trigger finger and put the safety back on.

"That was terrific, Cal," Marilyn said. She'd filmed the whole thing.

"That goddamn bear's got my rod!" Cal shouted. "Stop him, goddammit!"

"Goddammit yourself!" Bill shouted back. "Do you know how close you came to getting mauled? Now just shut up!"

Nobody told Cal to shut up. "That outfit cost me $500 and I intend to get it back!" he yelled back at the pilot. "You're responsible—you go get it!"

Bill grabbed hold of the man and spun him around. Cal was heavier, but Bill stood three inches taller. "I told you not to start fishing," Bill shouted in his face. "You lost the rod because of your own stupidity, and I'm not about to follow that bear into the alders looking for a damn fishing pole, no matter what it cost—and no one else is going to either. Now, get back to the plane—I've had it—we're leaving."

15

Janet wasn't one to put things off. As soon as she'd satisfied herself that all was well at the lodge, Charlie was all right, and dinner preparations moving along on schedule, she confronted Cal in the lounge. He was pouring himself a drink. She grabbed the glass out of his hand and slammed it back on the bar. "Pick up your things and get out," she told him, a glint of steel in her eyes.

"What's that brother of yours been telling you, ma'am?" Cal didn't believe her.

"He didn't have to tell me a thing—I was there, remember, and saw it all myself. Now, get out!"

"It's almost dinner time," Marilyn chipped in. "Where can he go this time of night?"

Janet turned on her in a flash. "This doesn't concern you, Marilyn, so just keep your mouth shut. The only reason we put up with you is because of our contract, so don't push it."

Marilyn shrugged, looked at Cal, and sat down on a sofa to watch.

"Don't worry, little lady," Cal said to her. "I'll talk to Charlie about it."

"No, you won't," Janet told him, moving across the room to block his way. "Charlie's resting, and will not be disturbed!" She waved a finger in his face. "You've got your own plane. Go anywhere you want to, but you're not staying here tonight," and she pointed to the door. "Now, get moving before I have my brother throw you out." She was mad enough to try it herself. Bill had never seen her so upset.

"You can't throw me out, ma'am," Cal just laughed at her. "I already paid for a whole week."

Janet was waiting for that—she shoved a check into his shirt pocket. "There's your deposit, minus one day's fishing. Now, out! Your bags are already packed and on the porch!" Janet had thought of everything. When Bill and John stood up, Cal headed for the door.

"Come on, Cal. I'll drive you," John offered, walking after him.

"You'll be sorry for this, Bascomb!" Cal said as he strode out. "I'll get you if it's the last thing I do."

John returned half-an-hour later while they were at dinner. "I took him over to Ike's," he said, as he pulled back his chair to join them. "That's where he asked to go and I couldn't see any reason why not."

"Who's Ike?" Marilyn asked.

"Who cares," her husband snorted.

"I care," Marilyn snapped. "Cal got us some great footage today, and I appreciate it even if you don't." She turned back to John. "Who's Ike?"

"Ike Sherman. He owns The Sportsman Lodge across the bay."

"I don't like it," Charlie said. "I wish he'd gone back to Anchorage, or any place else. That man's trouble, and so is Ike and Randy—and so is Cassius. I've been watching that bear since he was one of Miss Paine's cubs seven years ago, and Ike's people have been feeding him for a couple of years now—the whole situation's bad."

"Maybe we'd better fish someplace else," Bill said.

"I'd feel more comfortable," Charlie agreed.

"I won't!" Marilyn said, eyes flashing, chin stuck out a mile. "We're just getting familiar with that river and the conditions of light we have to work with there. Why start someplace new?"

Malcolm finally spoke up. "If Charlie and Bill think it's too dangerous on the Kamishak River, we ought to go somewhere else," he said.

"No!" Marilyn almost shouted at her husband. "Today is the first day we've seen a large bear on the stream. That's what the producers want, that's what they're paying us to film." Then she turned to Charlie. "I'll agree only if you guarantee we'll see a larger bear at another stream; The Warden for example."

Charlie knew that was unlikely. The larger boars usually stayed out of sight along the salmon rivers; fishermen and guides see their tracks sometimes, so they know they're still around, but those bears don't like to mix with humans. Older and wiser, they'd learned how to survive, and neither Charlie nor John had seen The Warden along a salmon river in over 10 years.

"I can't guarantee that," Charlie said.

"Then we're going back to the Kamishak River," Marilyn said. "And if you won't take us, I'll go over and hire Ike to take us—and send you the bill!"

Marilyn finally touched Charlie's soft spot. He threw up his hands in disgust. "Okay, okay, Marilyn, we'll play it your way tomorrow." He stood up and stalked out of the room.

Light winds, blue sky, and sunshine prevailed as Bill circled the river the next morning, first to inspect the landing area for logs and stumps that might have moved, the second pass to locate the fish. John was watching too; neither of them saw many salmon in the crystal-clear water of the lower pools, meaning that not many had come in on last night's tide.

That's not abnormal. Sometimes the salmon come in on every tide, sometimes on every other tide. After the run peaks, they might miss two or three days in a row.

"High tide isn't until noon today," John said. "Maybe the fish will show then."

"Maybe, but let's try upstream first," Bill said, and banked the plane to head upriver.

"The hell with the fish," Marilyn shouted from the back of the plane. "What about the bears?"

"No fish, no bears," John said. That shut her up for a while.

They found a large school of salmon a mile upstream from the river's mouth, a place where the river had split into three braids. The center braid was the largest, flowing between a 50-foot wide, gradually sloping beach on one side and a steep bank covered with willow and alder trees on the other. The beach side gradually sloped away under water, and it looked like it was about six feet deep along the far bank. Hundreds of gray-backed salmon were holding their positions all over the braid. They didn't see any bears but Bill knew they'd show up soon enough. Pointing out the place to John, he returned to the mouth of the river and landed in their usual place. He beached the airplane, tied it down, and they started walking upstream. Twenty minutes later, they were standing on the gravel bar they'd seen from the air, looking at a thousand salmon.

Ben, Malcolm, and John fished for an hour while

waiting for the first bear to appear, releasing each fish carefully back into the river. Marilyn walked up and down the beach kicking stones and muttering to herself.

John was just about to wade out to the middle of the stream, when a 600-pound sow, her muzzle whitened with age, emerged from the brush three hundred yards upstream. Two yearling cubs followed her, each weighing about 250 pounds. The sow walked slowly along the beach, then down to the water where she stopped just before reaching a two-foot-deep channel. Her front feet were only inches deep in the water, but her head was poised over the channel and her eyes watched the stream intently. She stood there as still as a statue—a solitary, inanimate, unmovable object at the edge of the current.

"Recognize her, John?" Bill asked.

"I think it's old Blondie," he said, returning to the beach. "I haven't seen her in a couple of years—thought she died of old age."

"She looks like she has arthritis, the way she walks," Malcolm said, reaching for his camera.

"She always walks like that," John said. "She's just cautious. And she doesn't like company, especially when she has cubs."

"Just don't let her fool you, Malcolm," Bill warned him. "She can move as fast as any other grizzly when she has to."

The salmon darted away from Blondie when she first entered the water, but the longer she stood there, the more they started to move back toward the channel she was watching. Bill could see she'd done this before; all her movements seemed deliberate. Bears learn where they can catch fish and where they can't; Bill and John had stumbled on Blondie's latest fishing hole.

"I've got to get closer," Marilyn said. "She's got her back to me and I can't get anything worthwhile at this distance." She started to move toward the bears when John caught her.

"Marilyn, I know that old sow," he said. "We're lucky she's as close as she is. You try to move any closer and she'll take her cubs to the next gravel bar upstream."

Marilyn frowned at John, but didn't try to move any closer.

"Watch Blondie, Malcolm," Bill said quietly, knowing what was coming, "and keep that camera running. Don't even blink or you'll miss it." Her cubs sat on the shore patiently waiting.

The river isn't home to the salmon. They're born there, spawn and die there, but they don't live there like the trout and char. They just pass through, heading upstream toward their spawning beds.

The other fish might know the danger, but to the salmon the motionless bear probably looked like just another rock or stump to swim around on their migration upstream. When one chanced to swim too close, Blondie's head darted underwater like a spear. Seconds later it reappeared, water dripping from her muzzle and a wriggling salmon clenched between her jaws. Carrying the fish ashore, she slowly and carefully killed and filleted it.

The cubs fought for the remains, filling the valley with their snarls and growls as they rushed at each other, biting and chewing, rolling over and over in and out of the water. The cub who lost trotted off and waded into the river 50 feet downstream.

First, it charged into the stream at the nearest salmon but the fish streaked into deeper water out of danger. Disappointed, the cub swam across to the opposite shore and climbed up the bank. Blondie sat down to watch from the gravel bar, scratching her neck with a hind foot.

The water was only a few inches deep on the near side, but the channel was four feet deep where the cub had crossed. The bank was a good six feet high; from the top, the young bear looked down into the water and saw the dozens of large salmon holding in the quiet water near the shore.

Leaping off the bank on top of the fish, the yearling created a cannonball-sized splash. Water flew everywhere. Dozens of salmon streaked away from the explosion, their massed bodies creating a wave on the surface. When the water smoothed out, the hungry cub climbed back up the bank again.

Following the school of fish, the cub dove in again. Again unsuccessful, it climbed back up the bank, trotted a few more feet upstream, and plunged into the water a third time.

"If he keeps doing that, he'll eventually get one," Bill laughed. "Keep an eye on him, Malcolm."

"What do you know that I don't?" Malcolm asked.

"That cub's slowly moving the school of fish upstream. Every time he jumps in and scares them, they move forward another 20 feet. Now look upstream; see how the river gets shallower up there. If he jumps on the fish there, he'll get one."

"Does he know what he's doing?"

"He's a young bear. Who knows?" John said.

The cub was tireless. Jump, climb back out, jump again, climb back out, it leaped into the river five more times, moving upstream on each jump. It finally caught a salmon, pinning it to the bottom with its front paws. Sitting down in two feet of water, the bear broke the salmon's back in its jaws and started to eat, holding the fish firmly between its two front feet.

When the cub finished his fish, he climbed back up on the bank to start again, but just then old Blondie stood up and ambled off upstream. The cub swam back across the river to follow her. Next year it would be on its own.

At noon, Marilyn wanted to go back to the mouth of the river to see if any fish had entered on the noon tide. Malcolm agreed, so Bill didn't have much choice but take them; John packed up the remains of their lunch and followed them as they navigated the various gravel bars and bear trails leading toward the airplane. Several fish were leaping and slashing on the surface of the river when they got there; for every salmon they saw jump, Bill and John knew there were dozens more underwater.

Randy also found them. About an hour later, he circled, landed, and beached his airplane next to Charlie's Beaver.

Bill had a good idea who the fisherman was in Ike's plane. As soon as Marilyn saw Cal, she rushed over to say hello. Cal assembled his fishing rod while they talked; he'd either borrowed one from Ike or bought another at the local store. "You stick around, pretty lady, and we'll really get some good pictures of bears today," he said, and waded into the water.

Cal quickly hooked his first fish. Backing up onto the beach, he skidded it 20 feet up the gravel before he stopped reeling. When Randy whacked it on the head with a large stick, blood from the gills gushed out onto the gravel. Bill walked over.

"Afternoon, Randy."

"What do you want, Bascomb?" he said. He had a large pistol strapped to his waist; Cal's fancy hunting rifle was propped against a log.

Bill's own rifle was still in the airplane. He'd taken Charlie's advice: Don't carry a weapon unless you think you'll have to use it. That puts you on a more equal basis with the bears and will affect how you act around them. Bill had been a little uncomfortable with the idea at first, but had slowly adapted to it as his experience along the salmon streams increased.

"It looks like we'll be here together the rest of the day," Bill said. "Thought I'd see if we could work together, maybe keep the fish blood in the river instead of on the beach."

"We'll fish any goddamn way we want to and I'll clean 'em any goddamn way I want to," Randy said. "Now get the hell away and leave me alone."

Bill shrugged and left. Fish blood all over the beach would attract every bear on the river eventually. It was just a matter of time; almost on schedule, Cassius showed up 20 minutes later. Wandering along the beach, he sniffed his way to the fresh salmon blood like a beagle on a rabbit's trail. When he started licking at the gravel, Randy rushed at him, shouting, cursing, finally firing a shot into the beach in front of the bear's feet. Gravel and sand showered the bear's head and chest as the bullet bit into the stones. Cassius sprinted back into the brush.

But he didn't stay away long, and Cal had a fish on his line when Cassius returned. It was a large salmon that was putting up a terrific fight, tearing all over the river trying to shake the hook, and had stripped over a hundred yards of line off Cal's reel. When it started thrashing violently on the surface, Bill and John both knew that Cal had foul-hooked the fish, either in the stomach or the side or near the tail; it was no longer swimming like a fair-hooked fish.

When Cassius saw the struggling fish, he charged into the river after it, lunging through the shallow water with spray flying. Cal kept the tension on his line and the salmon continued to thrash; seconds later Cassius grabbed the fish in his mouth.

"Hold him, Cal!" Marilyn shouted from the beach, her camera taking it all in. "Set that hook!"

Cal lifted his rod in a surging arc, straining the line almost to the breaking point. Cassius bolted away in a dash toward the shore, still clenching the fish in his mouth. "I can't hold him, Randy," Cal shouted. "He's taking all my line."

"Tighten the drag!"

"It is!" Cal yelled. A few seconds later, the line snapped and Cal staggered back, his rod straight again. Cassius galloped up the bank and disappeared into the alders with his prize.

"Hey, Marilyn," Cal shouted. "Did you get all that on film?"

"Every bit, Cal," Marilyn shouted back. "That's about the funniest thing I've ever seen—a man fighting a bear with a fishing pole!"

16

Charlie met the airplane when they landed. He asked John to drive the others to the lodge in the van, then sat on the floats while Bill refueled the Beaver from the 500-gallon tank mounted in the back of his pickup truck. The plane carried 95 gallons of gasoline in its three belly tanks.

"Your plan didn't work too well today, Charlie," Bill said. "I hope you've got something better for tomorrow." Then he told him what had happened when Cal and Randy showed up on the river.

Charlie stared at the water between the floats. When Bill finished, he heard him mutter, "Sons-a-bitches."

"You got anyone particular in mind?" Bill asked.

"The lot of 'em," he said. "Ike, Randy, Cal, Marilyn,

even Malcolm. They're trouble; maybe we shouldn't have taken that contract in the first place."

"But you did." Bill said, capping the front tank and shifting the nozzle to the center one. He'd never agreed with the idea but was supporting their choice, once made.

"And we'll see it through," Charlie said. "Only one more week."

"We've got to figure out a way to keep Marilyn away from Cal."

"I've been thinking about that, too," Charlie said. "How deep is the river now?"

"It's been dropping a few inches every day," Bill said. "The channel where we land is about five feet deep at low tide, but half-a-mile upstream you can wade across in hip boots. Why?"

"We're running short on gas for the plane," Charlie said, nodding toward the tank in the truck. "That's the last of it until the fuel barge arrives next week. We could have some gas flown in but that costs too much, so I'm going to send you back to the Kamishak with the whole group again tomorrow."

"Charlie, you have to be kidding. That's just asking—"

"Wait, let me finish," Charlie said. "Tie the plane up on the beach side, like you always do. Then, if Randy shows up, load everyone back into the plane and taxi over to the other side. Ben can catch just as many fish over there and the photographers can take all the pictures they want. The bears walk up and down both banks, don't they?"

"Marilyn won't like it," Bill said, smiling. He liked the plan already. "I heard her tell Cal she'd see him there tomorrow."

"She'll see him, all right—across the river," Charlie said, a grin spreading across his face, too. "Now, if you're finished fueling, let's get back for dinner. We've got fresh salmon again."

The next morning, Bill beached the plane at his usual

spot. A brisk offshore wind was blowing from the snow fields high in the mountains. Cooler air moved down the valley and out to sea; instead of sea weed and salt water, the smell of trees and tundra and wildflowers on the hills to the west filled the valley.

Ben and Malcolm started fishing, John lit a fire to start a pot of coffee, and Marilyn fussed over her cameras while waiting for the bears to show up. Bill sat on a log and watched for bears until Randy arrived about an hour later, landing and beaching his plane next to the Beaver.

"Okay, load your stuff in the airplane; we're moving across the river," Bill called to his group.

"Why?" Marilyn wanted to know. "I'm all set up here."

"We're not fishing with that crowd anymore," he told her, nodding toward Randy and Cal.

"I don't see why not," Marilyn argued. "It's a free country."

"Our party is moving across the river," he said. His voice was calm, the tone determined. "If you want to move to the Sportsman Lodge with your friend Cal, stay here. But if you want to stay at Charlie's place, you do what he says—and he says move! Got it?"

"We're moving, Marilyn," Malcom said.

Marilyn shrugged and picked up her gear. With everybody helping, they quickly loaded the Beaver, climbed aboard, and Bill taxied across the river to the opposite shore.

"Let's go over there," Cal called to Randy.

"The fishing's better here," Randy answered.

"If you come over here," Bill shouted, "we'll move back to your side. We can spend all day moving back and forth if you like. Your choice."

"I don't want to fish with you any more than you want to fish with me, Bascomb," Cal answered, then turned his back toward the river and began putting his own fishing rod together.

The bears stayed away all morning while Cal added fish after fish to his cooler. Ben and Malcolm each landed several salmon apiece, carefully releasing all but two back into the stream. John immediately killed the two fish they kept, wrapped them in a plastic bag, and stored them within the fish locker in the right float of the Beaver. Janet had issued standing orders to bring back some fresh salmon whenever they could.

By lunchtime, Cal's cooler was full of fish and Randy loaded it into his plane. About 3:00 p.m., Randy collected the rest of their catch in a burlap sack. When he had four or five salmon in the sack, he dragged them along the gravel to a short section of beach under a low bluff. He was a few hundred feet downstream of where Cal was fishing.

Bill had been watching Marilyn all day as she sulked around waiting for the bears to show up. Suddenly, he realized she was gone. "John, where's Marilyn?"

"Last I saw, she was going back into the bushes to go to the bathroom." John was standing next to Malcolm, who was busy fighting a large salmon.

"How long's she been gone?"

"I don't know," John said, as Malcolm finally landed the struggling salmon. He unhooked it and let it go. "Maybe half an hour."

"Marilyn!" Bill shouted, turning back to the riverbank. They were on the outside of a broad sweeping turn and Bill could see half-a-mile upstream and down. A two-foot-wide bear trail ran along the top of the bank, twisting and turning with the irregular indentations of the river. The bear trail was six feet above the water; the bank sloughed off at a steep angle to a narrow muddy shelf at the water line, then dropped another three to four feet to the bottom of the river.

Walking upstream toward the shallows, Bill finally spotted Marilyn on the other side of the river, walking down the bear trail on that side. She'd crossed over on the gravel bar upstream, out of sight of both Bill and John.

Across the river, Randy was kneeling on the sand, gutting Cal's fish, when Walleye appeared out of the brush. The bear walked toward the water, crossed the trail that Randy had used dragging the salmon, turned and followed it, nose sniffing the ground like a bloodhound. When the bear came to the steep bank, he climbed up and looked over the lip at the river. Randy was directly below him, a half-gutted fish in one hand, his knife in the other. Bill spotted the bear first.

"Watch out, Randy!" he shouted. "There's a bear right above you."

Randy looked up and saw Walleye—only 20 feet away from him. "Get out of here, you miserable son-of-a-bitch," he yelled, dropped the fish, drew his pistol, and climbed the bank to fire directly at Walleye. The shot missed Walleye's head by inches and he turned and ran, galloping up the bear trail that ran along the bluff. Randy fired five more shots, running along the trail in pursuit.

Marilyn was walking along the same bear trail toward the action. She couldn't see what was going on because of a small stand of willows between her and Randy.

"Marilyn, back up!" Bill shouted. "Get off the trail!"

Marilyn ignored him.

Walleye suddenly burst through the willows only 25 feet away from Marilyn, running straight toward her—almost 700 pounds of grizzly moving at 30 miles an hour! Marilyn did the only thing she could—she leaped off the bank into the river, still holding the video camera she'd been packing around all day. Protecting the camera with her body, she fell headfirst and backward into the water.

The bank was high, and the river was only two feet deep there; Bill knew she was in trouble. "John! Marilyn's in the river," he shouted, quickly shedding his jacket and charging into the water from his side.

Marilyn rolled into the stream and disappeared in the

swirling current, her head bobbing to the surface and disappearing again. "Drop the camera!" Bill shouted as he struggled across the current.

The water was up to his waist and getting deeper. He couldn't get a good foothold on the gravel, and the current was beginning to force him downstream. Lunging forward as the current carried Marilyn past, Bill grabbed her jacket and let the current carry them both downstream toward John, who was wading out to meet them.

Marilyn was unconscious, held up only by the flotation built into her jacket. John caught them just as Bill regained his own footing and together they carried her ashore.

Rushing to help, Ben immediately knelt down and examined her. She was still breathing. "Where's the nearest hospital?" he asked.

"Kodiak."

"Get her there! Fast! There's nothing I can do for her here."

17

Marilyn was still unconscious when they landed at Kodiak. Ben and Malcolm rode to the hospital with her in the ambulance; when Ben returned, he said she had a fractured skull and severe concussion. "It's good you two got to her when you did," he added. "She had water in her lungs, too."

They decided to spend the night in Kodiak and get an early start back in the morning. After breakfast, Ben, John, and Bill headed back to Iliamna; Malcolm stayed in Kodiak to be near his wife.

The flight was smooth all the way, with clear sunny skies and light winds; when they passed over the Kamishak River, John spotted salmon holding in the current just inside the river's mouth. When Bill circled again, they all saw them—hundreds of two to three-foot-long gray shapes silhouetted against the sandy bottom—and Bill knew they had to be fresh ones that had just come in on the morning tide. Since Ben had to get back to Anchorage tomorrow, he landed to give the doctor one more chance to fish.

As soon as the plane was tied down, Ben and John headed for the river. About a hundred feet apart on the gravel beach, they were standing in a foot of water and casting into the immense school of fish that was holding near the opposite bank. Half-an-hour later, Walleye walked out of the brush on their side of the river. As soon as he saw the fishermen, he started jogging up the beach toward them.

"Ben!" Bill shouted. "Walleye's coming!"

Ben was fighting a large salmon. His nine-foot rod was bent 90 degrees, his flyline a straight line from the rod tip to the fish. Just then, the fish broke water and thrashed on the surface. The minute Walleye saw it, he charged into the river.

The water was only two feet deep; Walleye splashed through it, spray flying up around his broad chest. When he got to where he'd seen the salmon thrashing, he stopped and peered down at the water to see where the fish had gone. Ben had broken it off and retreated, so there was nothing left for Walleye to see, but the bear stood up on his back legs, his big head swinging from side to side, still searching the surface of the water for the fish.

"The bear did that deliberately," Ben said, a few minutes later, watching Walleye walking away upstream still looking for the salmon. "He knew I had a fish on the line and came looking for it!"

"He must have seen your fish thrashing on the surface," Bill said.

"No," Ben insisted. "That bear knew, I tell you."

"You may be right," John said. "We've suspected it for

some time, but this is the first time I've actually seen a bear come right out into the river and wait downstream of a fisherman for a fish to thrash on the surface."

"A few days ago, we saw Cal fighting a fish that way," Bill said. "Cassius came out and grabbed that one; Walleye's no different—he's been educated too."

Then Bill heard a plane circling overhead and looked up to see Ike's 206. "Damn," he said, as Randy and Cal landed and started unloading tents, sleeping bags, boxes of food, fishing rods, and everything else they'd need to set up a camp.

Ben went fishing again, but John and Bill watched Cal and Randy carry all their gear above the high tide line and stack it in a large pile. Then they walked away toward the alders. "Now they're looking for a spot to set their tent up," Bill said, pouring another cup of coffee. "I bet they're going to camp in the alders."

Cal and Randy hadn't been gone five minutes when Cassius stepped out of the brush and trotted up to the pile of supplies, followed by Walleye two minutes later. The two bears started at opposite sides of the gear and chewed and clawed their way into the center—straight toward the T-bone steaks Cal and Randy had brought for their first dinner in camp. The pork chops, hamburger, bacon, and cold cuts were for later in the week. All the meat was unfrozen, wrapped in waxed paper, and stored in one of the cardboard boxes of food.

Cassius got to the meat first. Dragging out one of the steaks, he devoured it in one gulp and was just going in for another when Cal and Randy returned.

"Hey! Get out of there, you sons-a-bitches!" Cal shouted, running toward the two bears, waving his arms.

Both bears turned and looked at him for a few seconds, then turned back to their lunch. Cassius calmly lowered his head into the jumble of torn and damaged equipment and picked up another steak.

"That's our supper!" Cal wailed.

Randy pulled out his pistol and fired into the air; he knew a pistol was no match for an 800-pound grizzly. Cassius looked up as the bullets whistled over his head, but stood his ground; Walleye began to move away. "That damn bear's gonna eat the whole thing," Randy said.

"The hell he is!" Cal ran back to the airplane to get his rifle. "I'll teach them to mess around with me."

He loaded the rifle and walked toward the bears, yelling as he went; Cassius didn't budge but Walleye backed off some more. When Cal was 50 feet away, he raised the gun to his shoulder and fired. Hair and dust burst from Cassius's front shoulder. The bear fell over but immediately jumped up to his feet again. Loading another round, Cal fired again, this time hitting Cassius near the stomach.

Cassius had had enough—he whirled and bounded toward the alders as Cal fired again, this time aiming at Walleye.

"That'll teach 'em," Cal said, looking at the mess in front of him. "Hope to hell I killed 'em both!"

He could hope, but someone had to make sure. Bill started following Walleye's trail, but once he left the beach, Walleye's track was impossible to distinguish from those of the other bears that were constantly wandering back and forth through the area. If Cal had hit him, the wound hadn't bled very much. Bill lost his trail within minutes.

Cassius was a different matter. Cal had hit him broadside with his .300 Winchester Magnum on the first shot. He'd run away bleeding and the trail was easy to follow. First, Bill returned to the Beaver and got his own rifle, slipped a cartridge into the chamber, engaged the safety, and started to enter the brush.

"Wait a minute," Cal shouted, running after him. "What the hell do you think you're doing now, Bascomb?"

"Somebody has to find out if you killed that bear."

"What for? Let the goddamn thing rot out there. Who the hell cares?"

"Randy probably does," Bill said, "and you will too after it gets dark tonight and you get to wondering if there's a wounded grizzly on the loose."

Cal hadn't thought about that. "You don't think he's still alive, do you?"

"You want to come along and find out?"

Cal looked at the alders, thinking of the last time he'd been in the alders looking for a wounded bear with Bill. Then he looked across the river, then at Randy, then back at Bill. "You go to hell," he said, picked up his own rifle, and walked away.

Fifteen minutes later Bill found the dead bear. Cal had hit the thing in its heart—it ran 500 yards before running out of blood. After a quick inspection of the carcass, Bill headed back to the beach.

According to Alaska law, when a bear is killed out of season there has to be an investigation. If the investigating officer, normally an Alaska State Trooper trained in fish and wildlife protection, feels that the killing was not in self-defense or for the reasonable protection of property, he prepares a case for presentation before a magistrate or district judge.

A person found guilty can be fined, he can go to jail, he can lose his gun and the vehicle used for transportation, and he can lose his license to hunt in the state. First, however, the person responsible for the killing has to skin the bear and deliver the hide and skull to the nearest trooper.

"Are you kidding?" Cal yelled when Bill explained this to them. "I'm not going to skin that goddamn bear!"

"Maybe Randy will do it for you," Bill said, and started back to the plane with John and Ben. Cal and Randy had to work it out; Randy stood to lose his hunting license, too, and maybe even Ike's airplane if a court decided against

Cal. Bill had seen guides lose their planes to the State of Alaska before.

"Wait a minute, goddammit, Bascomb," Cal said, running after him. "Why does anybody else have to know about this?"

"Because I'm going to tell them," Bill said. His face was stern, his lips a thin line, his eyes squinted together. Bill hated to see a useless, unjustified act of violence, particularly when it affected grizzlies.

"Okay, okay," Cal said, and started to pull out his wallet. "So how much is it going to cost?"

"There isn't enough gold in the whole State of Alaska to stop me from reporting this," Bill said, then took a few steps back toward Cal and pointed his finger at him. "I'll see you run out of this state before I'm through; if not this way there'll be others, and that's a promise!"

18

Jim Roberts had been an Alaska State Trooper most of his life, cross-trained at the State of Alaska Department of Public Safety Training Academy in Sitka for both law enforcement duties and fish and wildlife protection. A sturdy six-footer, Jim had been assigned to the Iliamna Fish and Wildlife Protection Office for the last three years. With his flaming red hair, full beard, and deep booming voice, the trooper made his presence felt in any gathering. Jim and Charlie had been good friends for years; Jim and Bill had always gotten along pretty well considering Bill was a guide and Jim was a law enforcement officer—troopers automatically suspect all hunting guides of flagrant game violations, and with some justification. Ike started as a hunting guide!

Charlie called Jim to report the shooting as soon as Bill, John and Ben got back to the lodge. Jim came right over. Bill described what he'd seen while Jim took it all down in a little pad no bigger than his pocket. Then he asked Ben and John to tell what they'd seen, filling in one page after another. When Bill asked him why he used such a small pad, he said, "One pad per case. Each case is easier to keep track of that way; when I have to file my report, I know where to find all my field notes." Before he left, Jim asked Bill to meet him on the Kamishak River the following morning.

Bill arrived at 8:00 a.m., Jim a half-hour later, flying a Supercub on floats owned by the state. Cal and Randy were still in their four-man tent when Bill and Jim got to their camp. A few unwashed pots and dishes were scattered on the ground around the remnants of a fire pit; articles of clothing and the remains of a shredded sleeping bag hung on a clothesline strung between two trees.

Cal and Randy came out of their tent into the daylight, rubbing their eyes, still dressed in long johns. "What do you want?" Cal asked. He looked hung over; so did Randy.

"I have a report that one of you killed a bear here yesterday," Jim said. His immaculately pressed light brown uniform glistened in the morning sun, his campaign hat sat squarely on his head. "I'm here to investigate the shooting. Now, get some clothes on; I haven't got all day."

They waited while Cal and Randy got dressed, then Jim took their names. "Who shot the bear?" he asked.

"Cal did," Randy said. Cal gave him a dirty look.

"Then I'll take your statement first, Mr. Edgecombe," Jim said.

"What the hell is Bascomb doing here?" Cal wanted to know.

"Mr. Bascomb reported the shooting," Jim said. "I've asked for his assistance. Now, let's get on with it and show me what happened."

Cal led them to the place where the two bears had ransacked their gear, much of which was still there. Jim took pictures while Cal and Randy held up pieces of their torn, clawed, and bitten equipment.

"Damn bears. Look what they did to this." Cal said, holding up the remains of a large pack. The frame was bent and broken, the bag shredded and torn into three pieces.

"Now show me the carcass," Jim said. Again Cal led the way, or tried to, but he couldn't follow the trail so Jim asked Bill to lead. When they found poor Cassius's body, it lay on its stomach, with all four legs spread-eagled as if he had died in full gallop. A large, dark-red clot of blood stained the gravel around the chest; the small, charcoal eyes stared at the sky. Cal hadn't skinned it yet.

Jim took more pictures, then turned to Cal. "You say you killed this bear?"

"I told you I killed the son-of-a-bitch. It's one of the bears that tore up our camp."

"Then you have 24 hours to deliver the hide and skull to me in Iliamna."

Cal exploded. "I'm not skinning any goddamn bear—you want that hide, get Bascomb to do it!."

"Very well." Jim reached into a leather pouch on his belt and pulled out a set of handcuffs.

"Now, wait just a goddamn minute!" Cal's voice rose even higher as he backed away from the trooper. "What's that for? I'm no goddamn criminal!"

Jim reached into another pocket, took out a copy of the regulations, and thumbed through them until he found the proper page. "5 AAC 92.410, Taking Game in Defense of Life or Property," Jim read. "Game taken in defense of life or property is the property of the state…In the case of a brown bear, the hide and skull must be immediately delivered to the department. A surrendered bear hide (brown or black) must include the claws."

Jim folded up the regulations and stuffed them back into his pocket. "Now," he said, "you admit killing the bear, and I represent the state. So either you agree to comply with the law or I'll throw your own hide in jail."

"But I've never skinned a bear," Cal whined. "I don't know how."

"The regulations don't say anything about that," Jim said.

"So let Bascomb skin it!" Cal said, his voice stronger. "He's skinned hundreds of the goddamn things."

Jim turned to Bill. "Mr. Bascomb, do you want to skin this bear?"

"Not me." Bill could already smell the decaying carcass. Cassius had been feeding on salmon for over a month and his hide carried the stench of rotten fish. When the hide came off, the flesh would be even worse. Skinning a bear during hunting season when they'd been feeding on roots and leaves wasn't too bad; skinning one in the summer when they were eating salmon took a strong stomach. Cassius had already been dead almost 24 hours.

"Put out your hands, Mr. Edgecombe," Officer Roberts said, taking out the cuffs again.

Cal looked desperate.

"Guess you got to skin it," Randy told him. "Can't be too much harder than skinning a deer. I'll help."

"I can't stand here all day, Mr. Edgecombe," Jim said. "Make up your mind."

"All right, goddammit," Cal said, drawing out his sheath knife.

Jim described the process briefly, then said, "I'm going back to Iliamna, Mr. Edgecombe." Jim started to walk away, then, as if he just thought of it, turned back to Cal. "I'll expect you in my office this evening. Please don't disappoint me."

19

Later that fall, Bill told me that Malcolm and Marilyn Foster never returned to Iliamna. After Marilyn had been taken off the critical list, they moved her from Kodiak to Providence Hospital in Anchorage, the same place that treated Charlie. After another few weeks of recuperation, she was moved back East; Charlie and Janet boxed up all their things at the lodge and shipped them to their studio in Boston.

Bill was delighted when he found out that Marilyn was permanently out of his hair, but the needless shooting of Cassius was another story. Bill argued that the bear had been intentionally tempted into attacking the pile of food, but when Jim Roberts completed his investigation, he informed Charlie and Bill that it couldn't be proven.

"Stacking food on a beach known to be patrolled regularly by bears may have been stupid, but Cal and Randy were entitled to protect their belongings," Jim said. "Each case must be determined on its own merit. The protection of life and property was justified under our current regulations. I'd be laughed out of court if I tried to prosecute."

Cal left triumphant.

• • •

Before Bill returned to Kodiak that fall, he and John took guests to the Kamishak several more times, but they never saw Walleye on the river again. Miss Paine and Carlotta and Henrietta and all the others were there but Walleye had disappeared. Charlie figured the bear was either dead or had moved somewhere else to fish, but Bill had followed the tracks—he knew Walleye wasn't dead.

• • •

Bill spent Christmas at the lodge; when he came back he said that Charlie looked as fit as he'd seen him in years. Charlie even thought he might beat the odds and get his medical renewed, but in January the Federal Aviation Administration put an end to that kind of thinking. Once you've had a heart attack, a pilot's commercial flying days are over—no exceptions, especially for a man almost 60 years old!

Charlie took the grounding philosophically; after all, he was still alive and could go fishing occasionally, so he poured more of his energies into his job as the chief mechanic at their lodge. With Janet's encouragement, he even started taking a nap in the afternoon. The thing that bothered him most was having to hire a youngster to fly the Beaver—anybody under 30 was a youngster to Charlie, it didn't matter how many hours you had in the air.

Bill would have stayed in Kodiak flying the Goose that next summer if Charlie hadn't called.

Bill had just returned from a round-robin flight: Kodiak, Old Harbor, Akhiok, Karluk, and return, in early June. After beaching the old amphibian, he chocked the wheels on the ramp, flushed the hull down with fresh water to wash the salt off, and returned home. The phone rang as he was cooking his dinner.

"We've got a problem," Charlie said, after the usual report on the family's health. "Your buddy, Cal, bought the Sportsman Lodge from Ike this spring."

"My buddy, hell," Bill grumbled, but there was something else. Charlie wouldn't waste a phone call just to tell him that.

There aren't any special regulations for operating a fishing lodge in Alaska; all a person needs is a $50 business license issued by the state. There aren't any residency or apprenticeship requirements like those established for the hunting guides; Cal can live in Alabama for eight months and Alaska for the summer and operate the lodge legally. Alaska has a multi-million dollar industry operating within its borders without a shred of regulation to govern it.

"There's more," Charlie continued. "Cal also bought Ike's airplane, then he fired Randy a week ago and he's doing his own flying now. He's trying to crowd us out."

"What do you mean, trying to crowd you out?" Bill asked.

"He flies around looking for our plane, then lands nearby. When he finds our group of fishermen, he walks back and forth across the riffles and pools and scares all the fish. The kid I hired is a good enough pilot, but Cal's a bully, and the pilot doesn't know how to handle him. John's getting the same treatment."

"Can't Jim Roberts do anything?"

"He's been called to Naknek for a month. The Troopers are expecting trouble with the commercial fishermen this year."

The word had already spread to Kodiak. The price that

the canneries had offered for salmon had dropped so low that the Bristol Bay fishermen had threatened to strike.

"What can I do to help?" Bill asked.

"If we offered to match your salary, could you come over and do some flying for a while?"

"I brought him up here in the first place, so he's my problem, too," Bill said. "I'll see if I can get a furlough for a month. The Airways won't like it, but they have another pilot who can handle most of their flying. Look for me in a few days."

Bill's Cessna 180 was already in the water; the next day, he was airborne for Iliamna, once again flying over the familiar terrain surrounding the Kamishak River and Dream Creek. On a grassy, flat-topped ridge overlooking Dream Creek he spotted a large bear; when he flew lower and slowly circled, he saw that it wasn't a single bear—it was two of them, coupled like a pair of husky dogs, with a large dark male on top of, and slightly behind, a brownish-tan female. As Bill flew around the coupled pair, Walleye turned his head to watch the plane. Locked together with the sow, that's about all he could do.

"Walleye's alive," Bill said when he landed. John had come down to the pond to greet him. "He's moved back to Dream Creek."

"Yeah, we know." John didn't sound too happy about it. "He's already gotten into trouble over there—and he's not as friendly as last year."

Later that evening, Charlie, John, and Bill were sitting in the lounge with cups of coffee. "Are you sure it was Walleye you saw on top of that sow, and not The Warden?" Charlie asked.

"About as sure as I could be at 70 knots and 200 feet," Bill answered.

Charlie thought about it for a few seconds, then asked, "See any salmon in Dream Creek?"

"Nope."

"Isn't it a little early for the salmon, Dad?" John asked. "It's only the 28th of June."

"Maybe so," Charlie answered. "They usually show up during the first week in July."

"What happens if the salmon are late?" Bill's curiosity was aroused.

"The bears don't like it; they're hungry and expect to get fed on time," Charlie said. "Do you remember the last time they were late, John?"

"You mean the year I graduated from high school?"

"That's the time," Charlie said. He started to grin and turned to Bill. "You see, Bill, John was sweet on a little girl over in Kokhonak. What was her name? Alicia?"

"Damn, here comes that story again," John said, and walked toward the door. "I'll go meet the commercial flight and bring back the new guests."

"There's three of them," Janet said, sliding past her son. She walked to the coffee urn and drew a cup for herself before sitting down to join them.

"And you know very well what her name is, and her mother's and father's name," John called back to his father before he left. Charlie had touched a sore spot in his son's hide.

"You must be talking about Alicia again," Janet said, after John left.

"Not exactly," Charlie said. "Bill asked what happens around here when the salmon are late. I was about to tell him when John jumped up and left."

"You know he's still carrying a torch for that girl," Janet said, "and when she went off to college and married that engineer it almost broke John's heart."

"Well, anyway, there's nothing we can do about that, but let me get on with the story," Charlie said. "The sockeye salmon were very late, and the bears were getting hungrier by the day. You know, they continue to lose weight even after they come out of hibernation. Vegetation doesn't give them enough of whatever it takes to start gaining weight."

"It takes salmon, we know," Bill said.

"Well, anyway, The Warden was about Walleye's age then, maybe six or seven years old," Charlie continued. "The big fella left the hills by Dream Creek looking for food; he probably checked the whole length of the Gibraltar River and ended up on the shore of Lake Iliamna, not far from Kokhonak. He still couldn't find any salmon, but he did find Arkady's dog team staked out near their cabin at the mouth of the river."

"Arkady and Lucy Wassillie are Alicia's parents," Janet explained. Charlie nodded, then went on with his story.

"At first, Arkady only missed a couple of puppies, the ones that weren't old enough to chain up yet, but when the bear killed and carried off Arkady's lead dog—chain, stake, and all—they called us for help. John and I went right over."

Charlie sipped at his coffee; he'd long-since given up on the decaffeinated kind and was enjoying the real stuff again. "We decided to sit up all night at the dog yard and wait for the bear to show up again; Arkady and I sat watching the mouth of the river where the bear's tracks were the freshest, John and Alicia at the other end. That way we had all 15 dogs staked out between us, each of them on a ten-foot-long chain."

"Did the bear show?"

"I'm getting to that," Charlie said. "We sat there until well after midnight, not making a sound; the dogs settled down and slept, Arkady and I sat silently watching in the half-light. I don't know what John was doing although he swears he was watching all the time. Anyway, about 2:00 a.m. I heard a thump, then wood crashing. The sounds came from John's direction, and the only thing I could think of that was built out of wood over there was Arkady's smokehouse. I asked him what he had in his smokehouse."

"We heard another splintering crash from the same direction, and I asked him again. He was reluctant to say so, but he finally told me he'd just killed a caribou a few days ago, out of season, of course, and he'd hung the quarters in the smokehouse. I shouted at John to cover the smokehouse; then Arkady and I started running down the dark, twisting path through the dog yard leading toward it. Arkady had a flashlight lashed to his shotgun, and took the lead; I stumbled along behind him with my rifle, dodging the tethered dogs, all of them wide awake and howling mad. They'd smelled the bear, and didn't like being tied up—God, what a racket they made.

"When Arkady and I got to the smokehouse, we saw The Warden step out of a large hole he'd torn in the wall, turn, and lope away with a big hind-quarter of meat in his mouth. Arkady fired both barrels at the bear but I couldn't shoot because he was in front of me. Anyway, the bear got away with the meat."

"What happened to John?" Bill asked.

"John was too busy to shoot a bear," Charlie said, smiling again. "He and Alicia got there a few minutes after all the excitement was over."

"He's still a little embarrassed about it," Janet said, "and Charlie keeps on stirring the pot." She rolled her eyes. "You know how Charlie is when he's got something on someone."

"So, what happened to the bear after that?"

"Nothing, as far as we know," Charlie said. "The salmon came in a few days later and the next time we saw The Warden, he was feeding along Dream Creek as if nothing had happened."

It was Bill's turn to change the subject. "What's the fishing like at Dream Creek this year, Charlie?"

"So far, so good," he said. "We've sent three groups over there this spring and they all caught a lot of trout—until Cal showed up. Two of our guests got so mad that they left early."

"Left early! What the hell was he doing?"

"He walked right through a pool where we were fishing," John said, walking back into the lounge. "When I told him to get the hell out of there, he gave me the finger."

"And now he's set up a camp over there," Charlie said. "He dropped off two guys yesterday; it looked like they were going to stay for a while."

"And Walleye's back," John added. "I saw him yesterday on the creek."

It wasn't just campers Charlie was worried about, or even Walleye; it was the long-term results of constant confrontations between humans and bears. Hunting guides never worried about such things; they either shot the bear or let it go. Simple. But with fishermen, Charlie had to deal with the bears every day.

Camping along a river doesn't have to be confrontational, or even disturbing to the bears. But they'd already seen how Cal did it, and he wasn't the only one; several air taxies in Anchorage also flew people into the bush to set up camps. Smaller air charter operators in the villages, like the local Skytaxi, did the same. Charlie had thought of doing it himself a few years ago but he'd decided against it. As Janet had said, he'd probably work up an ulcer worrying about them out there alone, wondering if they were getting into trouble. Dropping people off in the wilderness can go well, but it can also be disastrous.

Charlie's three new guests wanted to go rainbow trout fishing; the following day he sent Bill to Dream Creek with them. When they arrived, Cal's two campers were still in their tent, a flimsy-looking, two-man, nylon job with a yellow fly, so Charlie's guests had the stream to themselves for a while. They found a fresh school of rainbow trout near the outlet and stayed there.

Bill sat on a stump and watched; an hour later he smelled burning kerosene. The campers had gotten up at last and started a fire.

"You want bacon and eggs this morning?" one of them said to the other. Their voices sounded loud and clear in the crisp morning air.

"Let's use up the bacon."

Five minutes later the odor of frying bacon came drifting downwind, and Bill wondered if anyone had told them what to do with the grease. He thought of going over and telling them but decided against it; shortly afterward, his group wanted to go upstream so he guided them along the well-worn bear trail to some of the pools and runs that John had showed him last season. An hour later, Cal flew in and picked up the campers; four hours later, Bill returned to the beach, inspected the deserted campsite, and found that a bear had already been there before him.

The campers had poured their bacon grease on the ground. The place was now marked by a two-foot circle of dirt. All the grass had been chewed away and the dirt beneath it licked smooth. A few feet away from the grease-licking was a ragged, two-foot-deep hole, where they'd buried their garbage. The bear had dug it all up, and the inedible remains—paper, plastic, and a few tin cans—were scattered around the camp. Taking a plastic bag from his gear, Bill picked up the trash, stuffed it in the bag, and carried it to his own plane.

Both Bill and Charlie had cleaned up a lot of trash in the past but this was the first time they knew exactly who'd left it. "Take it over to him," Charlie said. "It might be a good way to let Cal know you're back."

Bill added a few bricks to the bag of trash and threw it into the back of the truck; then he drove over to the Sportsman Lodge. Pulling up in front, he honked the horn until Cal opened the door and stepped out on the porch.

"Your guests left this on Dream Creek today," Bill said, tossing the bag onto the porch. It landed with a loud thump and broke open, strewing trash all over Cal's feet.

"Goddamn you, Bascomb, are you back here again?" Cal yelled. "Get off my land!"

Bill climbed back into the pickup truck as Cal jumped down off the porch. He picked up a handful of gravel and threw it at the truck as Bill drove away.

20

Bill woke up at 4:00 a.m. thinking about Cal and Walleye and Dream Creek; at 6:00 he joined Charlie, Janet, and John for coffee in the lounge. Breakfast was still an hour away and they had the place to themselves.

"I think we should put a camp on Dream Creek," Bill said, balancing a cup on his knee.

"What?" Janet said, her brown eyes wide open, her lips slightly parted. She and Charlie set their coffee down on the small table between their twin recliners; John's cup hung suspended inches in front of his mouth, a puzzled frown on his face. Charlie just looked at Bill.

"Hear me out on this," Bill continued, now looking at Charlie. "We know that Walleye's over there. He'll probably hang around all summer and so will several other bears once the salmon are in. And, incidentally, I saw the first dozen salmon schooled at the mouth of Dream Creek yesterday."

"That'll attract bears to the mouth," Charlie said, "and, if we put a camp over there, that's where it has to go." His voice was quiet, contemplative.

"It'll have to be a sterile camp," Bill said. "No cooking odors, no open food containers, sack and haul the garbage every day, and so on, but if you want me to keep an eye on Cal, I have to be over there."

The room was quiet. The sun peeked over the hills to the east and bathed the room in a rosy glow as they all sat and looked at Bill. "Ben Thompson is arriving tomorrow," John said, a minute later. "I'll bet he'd like to camp on Dream Creek. He could fish 24 hours a day."

"You can't do it all yourself, Bill," Charlie said. He wasn't one to get distracted from the main issue.

"I was counting on using John to watch things at the camp when I have to fly. He's camped in bear country enough to know what to do, and what not to do."

"How about it, John?"

"Okay with me, Dad," John said, shrugging. "I can get along with the bears; I'm not so sure about Cal." Then he turned to his mother. "What do you think, Mom?"

"Just be careful," Janet said, looking at her brother. "I know Charlie asked you to help out with Cal, and I supported him on that, but we don't want any more trouble than we already have." She stood up and headed for the kitchen. As the door closed, Bill smelled bacon frying, something he wouldn't have at a sterile camp.

So it was unanimous. Bill flew their equipment to Dream Creek the following day: two tents, cots, sleeping bags, and a myriad of other items. The campsite he selected was a smooth gravelbed in a clearing surrounded by alders and willows on three sides; the fourth side faced Gibraltar

Lake, 100 feet away. The site was 200 yards from the river, where they expected most of the bears to congregate.

Bill and Ben set the tents up 50 feet apart in the clearing; one tent for cooking, the other for sleeping. All of their food was stored in bear-proof containers, barrellike steel cans with lids that were held on with heavy bolts, and Bill gave Ben strict orders—they only opened the cans when it was time to eat, and resealed the cans when they were done.

"And one more thing," Bill said. "Don't bring any food into the sleeping tent."

After they'd set up the camp, they walked down to the mouth of the creek; hundreds of salmon were nosed into the current. Tomorrow there'd be thousands out there, stretching a hundred yards in all directions from the creek mouth. More salmon in the lake would bring more bears to the shore, and Bill looked around at their small clearing after they'd returned to camp. Willow and alder thickets crowded to within 50 feet of the tents. With Ben's help and a brush ax, Bill cleared out another 25 feet of brush all around the tents.

In a few more days the first salmon would leave the lake and migrate up the creek to spawn. Tens-of-thousands of others would follow over the next month; the fish put it off as long as they can, but they have to leave the protection of the deep water in the lake eventually and enter the shallow creek to find their spawning beds. That's where the bears can catch them.

Ben finally quit fishing at 11:00 P.M. and joined Bill in the tent. Always a restless sleeper, Bill woke up an hour later to the sounds of rustling and pawing. He folded back the door flap of their sleeping tent and looked out but it was too dusky to see clearly. Before he could find his flashlight, he heard a loud, ripping sound and then pots and pans crashing to the ground.

"What was that?" Ben asked, groggily, wiping the sleep from his eyes.

"Quiet, Ben," Bill said. "It sounds like a bear."

Moments later, the beam from his flashlight revealed a large, dark-colored bear among the ruins of their cooking tent. He'd knocked the whole thing down, poles and all, and was now ripping and tearing at everything within reach.

"Did you leave any food over there?" Bill asked, his voice low and calm.

Ben was silent for a minute. "Just a couple of candy bar wrappers," he said.

"Dammit, Ben, the candy may be gone but the smell's still on the wrapper," Bill said, a sign of irritation in the whispered reprimand. "He can smell it."

Walleye was intent on finding something to eat; he ripped and tore another five minutes; then the bear bit into an unopened can of soda.

Fizzzzzzzz.

"Damn, damn, damn," Bill said, still quietly. They'd brought a case of soda and a case of beer, and stored them both in the tent. It took Walleye half-an-hour to slurp up the contents of all 48 cans, then he walked away into the brush.

"How much beer does it take to get a bear drunk?" Ben asked.

"How am I supposed to know?" Bill said. He was tired and disgusted, and turned the light off. "Let's get some sleep."

"Turn that light back on!" Ben shouted, only a few feet from Bill's ear. "Turn it on! Turn it on!" He was frantically reaching for the lantern. "The bear's still out there!"

"Hey, Ben, calm down," Bill said, relighting the lantern. Ben's face was white, with beads of perspiration on his forehead. "I saw the bear leave, so relax."

"He might come back! What then?"

"I've got my rifle if we need it, so calm down, will you," Bill said. Ben had always seemed composed around the bears last year, but he'd only seen them in the daylight. Maybe that was the problem. Bill had little choice but to leave the light on for a while, at least until Ben got back to sleep again.

Two hours later the bear returned, and Bill heard him shuffling around the remains of the cooking tent again. Ben was sound asleep, snoring lightly.

Bill flashed the light at the bear to confirm that it was Walleye, then turned it off. He didn't want to arouse Ben, so he stayed inside the tent. There was enough daylight to see the outline of the animal without the flashlight.

Walleye pawed around the cook tent for a few minutes, then ambled slowly toward their sleeping tent. He approached so closely that Bill could hear him breathing; deep, rasping breaths, his great chest expanding and contracting like an enormous bellows, forcing air in and out of lungs several times larger than Bill's. His shaggy coat smelled of skunk and fish and rotted vegetation.

Walleye slowly walked around the tent—only 10 feet away. The smell left but the breathing and an occasional crunching leaf told Bill where he was. Once, Bill felt the tent shake as Walleye's foot pulled at one of the tie-down ropes.

Bill's own breathing stopped as he listened for noises outside, but the bear moved so quietly that once he left the tent, he couldn't hear anything more until Walleye returned to the remains of the cooking tent. He rummaged around it for another few minutes, rattled a pot or two, then all was silent again; when Bill flashed the light, the bear was gone. That time Ben didn't wake up—thank God! Bill thought. His own heart was pounding enough for the both of them.

Unable to get to sleep again, Bill quietly slipped out of the tent and surveyed the mess: ripped and torn tent, scattered and dented pots and pans, broken dishes, and dozens of aluminum cans with puncture holes in every one of them. When Ben got up an hour later, he found Bill stringing all the pop and beer cans on a long piece of nylon cord.

"What's that for?" Ben asked.

"Bear warning system," Bill said. "You can help by going down to the beach and filling that kettle with pebbles."

After Bill had strung all the cans, he inserted a few pebbles in each can. Then they strung the line from tree to tree completely around the camp. When Bill pulled it bowstring tight, the cans hung suspended two feet off the ground. Then he pawed at the string—like a bear might do it—and all the cans in that section rattled. Later in the morning, while Ben fished, Bill flew back to the lodge, got another tent, and rebuilt the camp.

Walleye came back that night but they were ready for him. This time Bill went to bed fully dressed; the second the bear touched the cord and set off the alarm, Bill leaped out of bed and ran, shouting, out into the opening between the two tents. Walleye's blurred shape disappeared into the surrounding brush. An hour later he reappeared and Bill surprised him again; that time he left for the night, and the next day's events lured him away from their campsite to the new one across the creek.

Bill and Ben were both upstream the following morning when Cal flew overhead, circled once, then landed in the lake. Ten minutes later they heard Cal take off, only to return in an hour. By the time Bill and Ben returned to their own camp, Cal had made four trips to Dream Creek. When Bill walked down to the lake for a bucket of water before supper, he counted six men at the camp and four others fishing in the lake near the outlet of the creek.

The next day, Charlie and Janet had two more guests arriving on the noon flight. Bill left Dream Creek early in the morning, taking Ben back to the lodge with him to take a shower and clean up. Then he flew Ben, John, and the new guests back to Dream Creek about 3:00 p.m. The floats had barely touched the beach when one of the campers ran down to the lake, launched a small rubber dinghy, and rowed over to Bill's side of the creek. Bill was still tying up the plane when the man ran up to him.

"I must go back to Iliamna at once," he said, speaking with a Scandinavian accent. The tall, fair-skinned man's jacket was unbuttoned, his hip boots were turned halfway down as though he'd just hurriedly put them on, and his eyes darted back and forth, up and down the beach.

"I'll take you when I go," Bill said. "It'll be a few hours."

"Right now!" the stranger insisted. His face was flushed, muscles flexed in both cheeks, his eyes bulging. "I must go right now!"

If they'd had an accident, or one of them was sick or injured, Bill would have had to leave the guests with John and help them out. Otherwise, he could wait. "Why are you in such a hurry?"

The man took a deep breath and slowed down. "My name is Okè, and I am the leader of that group of fishermen," he said, pointing at their campsite. His accent was strong and Bill had to listen carefully to understand, so he turned to face him squarely. The camper was standing with his back to the creek.

Bill introduced himself and shook his hand. The man held on tightly. "We are all from Sweden," he said. "I must get back to Iliamna immediately to talk to our pilot. We must leave this place as soon as possible."

As Bill pulled loose from his grip, he could see their campsite over the man's shoulder. Past their group of tents was a grassy hill about 300 feet high; as Okè talked, Bill watched a dark chocolate-colored bear walk over the crest of the hill and descend toward the tents.

"Excuse me, Okè," Bill interrupted the explanation. "There's a bear walking toward your campsite."

"Ach, that one again," he said, turning to look. Then he

ran down to the creek, shouting in Swedish and pointing, first toward the hill, then the beach, gesturing with both arms. Then, one of the two men still fishing ran down the beach to a small stump and untied a stringer of fish. He took one salmon off the stringer, tossed it farther down the beach, and then ran back to where his partner was.

The bear walked slowly down the hill and behind their tents. Bill lost sight of it for a minute as it made its way through the tangle of brush and alders near the shore, but picked it up again as it stepped out onto the sand.

"Walleye?" Ben asked, walking over to stand beside them.

"Who else?" Bill said. The bear walked slowly along the beach toward the two Swedes, picked up the salmon, and walked back into the brush.

"What the hell is this?" Bill demanded, grabbing Okè's arm and spinning him around to face him. "Feeding time?"

"That damn bear," Okè said. "He came yesterday, and I did what Cal told me to do—'Throw him a fish, he'll leave you alone.' Now the bear comes back every few hours and we have to keep feeding him. He's a pest; we can't eat, we can't sleep, and someone must keep fishing all the time so that we have enough salmon. We must leave this terrible place as soon as possible."

Bill decided that another few hours wouldn't make much of a difference. He flew Okè back with them, leaving John to watch the camp.

Bill brought Charlie's guests back to Dream Creek the next morning. The Swede's camp was gone, but Cal showed up with four guests an hour later. Cal and his party stayed by the lake all morning and fished at the creek mouth for the salmon. John and Bill took their guests upstream to fish for trout. Cal walked upstream by himself after lunch.

Bill was standing next to Ben when Cal rounded the corner downstream of them. Catching sight of Bill, Cal splashed his way across a shallow gravel bar and continued walking right into the pool where Ben was fishing. The water in the pool was only two feet deep but Ben had already hooked several trout there.

"Get out of the pool, Cal!" Bill shouted. "Can't you see this man's fishing here?"

"I'll go anywhere I damn please," Cal said. As he continued toward them, Bill walked out into the stream to head him off.

"I'll only say it one more time, Cal," Bill said. He walked right up to Cal and faced him from two feet away. The water surged around their knees. Bill was taller but 20 pounds lighter. "Stay out of our water!" he said sharply.

Cal tried to brush past him, their shoulders almost touching in the middle of the stream. Bill waited until Cal took a step, balancing on his left foot while he shoved his right leg against the two-knot current, then Bill lunged into Cal's chest with his right shoulder. Bill caught him by surprise, spinning him around on one leg, and Cal fell to his knees in the water, facing downstream and away from Bill. Before he could get up, Bill put his foot on his butt and shoved as hard as he could, sprawling Cal head first into the creek.

Bill backed off as Cal sat up. The current was flowing around him just like he was another rock or stump in the middle of the creek.

"That's your side of the river," Bill said, pointing across the creek. "This is mine. Cross it again and I'll do more than just give you a bath!" Bill turned around, waded ashore, and walked away. Ben followed him upstream to another pool full of fish.

Bill half-expected Cal to follow—he was big enough and strong enough to make a real fight of it if he wanted to—but he didn't. Half-an-hour later they heard Cal start up his engine and leave.

Two days later Bill and Cal met again on Dream Creek.

This time Cal had a sawed-off shotgun slung across his back when he moved past, but he stayed on the opposite side of the stream and walked by without looking at Bill. He wanted to make sure Bill saw the gun.

21

It's no wonder that bears flock to the salmon rivers of Alaska every summer. Six different sub-species of salmon mature at sea in the North Pacific Ocean, navigating through thousands of miles of open sea by use of the earth's magnetic field. Five sub-species: Chinook (king), Coho (silver), Sockeye (red), Chum (dog), and Humpback (pink), return to North America (the Cherry salmon migrates to Asia). The chemical implant each fry receives from the water in which it hatches eventually lures each mature fish back to its natal stream.

Bristol Bay produces the largest Sockeye salmon run in the world. Returns of 50 million fish have been recorded but the average is between 25 and 35 million. The Kvichak

River, which flows from Lake Iliamna to the sea, accounts for about half of the return each season.

The Sockeye salmon migration through Bristol Bay can last a month, and commercial fishermen catch half to three quarters of the returning fish each year. The salmon who escape the miles of gill nets stretched across their path in salt water, enter fresh water in June and July, swimming upstream through the Kvichak River in an unending flow, head to tail, sometimes three and four abreast along both banks. When the run is on, an unbroken string of fish stretches 60 miles from the tidal salt water of Bristol Bay to Lake Iliamna. Once the salmon reach Lake Iliamna, they separate and head toward their spawning streams.

Spawning takes place everywhere, but primarily within the streams that feed the large lake, from the creek mouths to the tiniest tributary upstream, in shallow water and deep, in the fastest flows and in pools where there is no current at all. But the majority of spawning is done in gravel where the stones average one-half to two inches in diameter and where there is a constant flow of water moving at about a foot every few seconds. The depth of water over the gravel can be as little as three to four inches or as deep as ten to twelve feet or more.

The spawning process is started by the female, who turns on her side and violently flips her tail up and down over the gravel, moving some of the stones aside to create a depression in the creek bottom. Repeating the process many times, she deepens the hole to a foot or more below the stream bed, and the loosened gravel washes downstream in the current. Called a redd, the hole will become a nest for about 3,000 eggs.

During egg laying, the male, or buck, takes a position directly downstream and over the hen. After the hen deposits a group of eggs in the slack current at the bottom of the redd, she gives way to the buck, who squirts a milky stream of milt over the eggs. The process is repeated until all the eggs have been laid and fertilized, after which the hen again moves to the upstream edge of the redd. With the same body motions that dug the hole, she showers it with gravel from upstream, thereby burying the eggs several inches below the flowing water.

All Pacific salmon die after spawning. Their carcasses remain in the stream and the protein of their decaying bodies provides the nutrient for their offspring to live on the following spring when the eggs hatch.

Once the salmon start spawning in Dream Creek, they become easy prey for the bears. Not only are the fish in shallow water, but they've changed colors, from gray backs and silver sides to bright red bodies and bright green heads. They look like a neon sign, all lit up, saying come catch me! Somebody asked Charlie once why the salmon change color. His answer: "So the bears can see 'em."

• • •

Walleye and his kin left both of the camps alone for a week. Then, several days after the spawning started, Charlie sent Bill back over to Dream Creek with another group of fishermen. John was at the camp.

Up to that time, Janet had packed all the food for the camp, but that morning there were too many distractions: three new guests arrived in their own airplane before breakfast and had to be checked in, the diesel generator ran out of fuel and shut itself off, and the kitchen stove ran out of propane. Breakfast was late. Janet was too busy to pack the lunches so she delegated the job to the housekeeper.

Bill picked up the cooler containing both their lunch and John's dinner of frozen hamburger and cheese, and headed for the airplane. When he and the guests arrived at the creek half an hour later, Bill left the lunch box on the beach near the plane, then John and Bill walked upstream with the fishermen. Shortly before noon Bill walked back to start lunch, asking John to bring the guests down in 30 minutes.

Bill walked past the tent and was headed toward the beach when he saw Walleye—with his nose in the lunch box. When the bear pulled it out to look at Bill he had a brick of cheese in his mouth.

Bill ran toward the bear, stopping only long enough to pick up a small branch from the stack of firewood John had collected. Shouting wildly, he threw it at Walleye but it sailed ten feet over his head. The bear jogged down the beach a hundred yards and sat down looking back at him.

Walleye'd torn the top off of the cooler; there were tooth punctures and deep, foot-long claw marks all over it. The hamburger was gone but a small pool of blood on the bottom marked where it had lain. The evidence was all there: the meat had thawed, the blood leaked through the wrapping and, unfortunately, the cooler wasn't sealed against escaping odors. Janet had always sealed the food in tight plastic containers before putting it in the lunch box. The housekeeper didn't.

The river was full of salmon and Walleye's belly was full and round—almost pear-shaped. He didn't need John's hamburger and cheese, or the sandwiches they'd brought for lunch, but he ate them anyway, leaving only a few apples and some cookies. He'd have gotten them, too, if Bill hadn't arrived.

After chasing the bear away, Bill set and lit the fire. At least they could have some coffee with their cookies. But he had a more serious problem than short rations for lunch. Walleye wouldn't go away!

John and the guests arrived back at camp shortly afterward, and they ate what was left of their lunch while Walleye sat along the beach a hundred yards away and watched. They could tell what the bear was thinking: he'd found a tasty morsel, been interrupted while eating, and wanted to dig around in that cooler for some more food—and he wasn't going to leave until he'd done it. Bill had to try and drive him away or John would have nothing but trouble all night. He picked up a branch and walked toward the bear.

"Get out of here, you big SOB!" Bill shouted, waving the branch and striking the ground in front of him with it. He walked toward Walleye with the branch, slapping it against the sand and shouting until the bear stood up and moved away another 50 yards. When Walleye sat down Bill moved toward him again, still shouting and waving the branch.

Walleye would let Bill get to within a hundred feet before he moved away, but he wouldn't go far. After three more attempts to drive him out of the area Bill returned to John and the others. "Pack up your things, John," he said. "I'll guide these guys the rest of the afternoon but we're going to move you back to the lodge tonight."

"What about the tents?" John asked.

"We'll leave the cook tent here, but take the sleeper and all the food with us."

"Even the canned food?"

"All of it, John. We won't have room for the cot and table but bring the stove and lantern. The pots and dishes can stay as long as they're clean."

"How long are we going to leave the tent up?" he asked.

Bill hadn't figured that out yet. So far, his theory had been right. The bears had left them alone for more than a week, but what would they do to an empty tent? With no food, no humans, no smells to tempt them, and the warning system still intact, Bill decided to find out. Charlie agreed after he'd been told what had happened.

The tent was still standing a week later even though there were nine adult bears and half-a-dozen cubs feeding along the creek. But on his next flight, Bill found the thing demolished, and he landed to investigate. A bear had torn through the rip-stop nylon exterior, shredded the built-in, heavy canvas floor, and collapsed the aluminum poles.

The bear had chewed pieces out of the sponge rubber

mattress and carried the remainder into the bushes, 200 feet from the tent. Bill and Charlie had always wondered why a bear would eat sponge rubber. Charlie'd even seen a grizzly chew the rubber bumpers off the front of a set of airplane floats once.

Bill picked up the mess, loaded it in the Beaver, and flew back to Iliamna. Another lesson learned; every time you think you've got the grizzlies figured out, they do something different.

22

Doctor Ben Thompson couldn't stay away from Iliamna. He'd returned to work ten days ago, but had enjoyed the fishing so much that he called for a fishing report every night since he'd left. Charlie invited him back for another visit; Ben arrived that evening.

"Where's the best place for rainbows?" Ben asked, settling into a comfortable sofa in the lounge. Charlie and Janet were sipping iced tea in their matched recliners, facing Ben. Bill was propped on a bar stool with his usual scotch and water.

"Dream Creek," Charlie said. "It's full of salmon and trout and bears."

"But no camp anymore?" Ben asked.

"We don't think it's safe to stay overnight anymore, but we're still fishing the creek in the daylight hours," Charlie said. "I'll have Bill take you in the morning if you like."

That's what Ben wanted to hear. Bill flew him and John to Dream Creek early the next morning; it was Bill's first trip over there since he'd cleaned up the camp five days ago. With the lack of rain, the water in the creek had been slowly dropping all month. The gravel bars were getting wider as the stream dropped; it was now shallow enough so that they could easily spot every trout in the creek while standing on dry land.

Ben and John fished their way upstream slowly, taking, then releasing a few fish out of each pool. Bill even fished a little with his new friend, but spent so much time watching for bears that he finally put his rod away and tagged along the shore, watching as the others fished. Walleye showed up shortly after noon.

"Bear coming, Ben," Bill called, loud enough for John to hear also.

"Where?" Ben asked. He and John were both downstream of Bill.

"Upstream. He just came around the bend, walking down the gravel bar. He's heading this way."

"What should I do?" Ben asked.

"Keep on fishing, for now," Bill said. The bears they'd seen approaching in the morning had all disappeared back into the alders to go around them, and reappeared on the stream 100 yards away. But this was Walleye. Bill kept his eyes on him.

The grizzly slowly plodded along the shoreline of a wide gravel bar. When Walleye looked up from the river and saw the three men a hundred yards downstream, he paused and stared at them. After a few seconds he looked back at the water, turned to look at Bill again, then continued moving in their direction.

"Whoa, Mr. Bear!" Bill called. "We were here first!"

Walleye continued moving downstream. "I don't think he's listening, boss," John said. He and Ben had walked upstream to join Bill.

The bear was still coming toward them, and Bill didn't like the looks of him—too rangy, too intractable. Walleye continued along the beach, caught the quick flash of a salmon as it darted across a shallow bar, and charged into the stream. Too slow and late to catch the shimmering fish, he returned to the graveled shoreline, showered the beach as he shook the water from his shaggy coat, and continued stolidly marching downstream.

"Ben, John, let's get out of here," Bill said. He led the way through the alders and away from the stream, then climbed a small knoll. The bear passed the spot they'd vacated moments before, sniffed at their tracks briefly, then continued walking along the riverbank.

They waited until the bear disappeared around the next bend, then returned to the creek. Ben fished without interruption for another hour, then joined Bill and John sitting on a log along the river bank. He sat down with a sigh and rubbed his casting arm.

"Sore?" John asked.

"Yeah, and my legs are tired," Ben said. "I need a break. You got any coffee?"

"Down at the plane," Bill said. He'd stopped carrying any food with them along the river, choosing to leave it either in the baggage compartment inside the plane or stowed in one of the pontoons.

Ben sighed, then smiled. "Walleye's been giving you more trouble, hasn't he."

"That's the understatement of the week," Bill said. "Walleye stopped acting like the other bears some time ago. He doesn't give a damn who's around him anymore, and he's lost his natural fear of humans. He runs people off the river, steals their fish, and breaks into their camps.

"I wonder if those campers down by the lake have had

any trouble?" John asked.

"Not yet." Bill had spoken to the campers briefly that morning while the others fished. Two Norwegians, they'd said, there to take bear and salmon pictures. Bill recalled mentioning it was a good place for both.

"If you've caught enough fish today, Ben, let's quit and get back to the beach," Bill said. "I think we ought to check on the campers again."

The Norwegians had set up their camp on the same site as the Swedes. They were using a single tent, with their three-day supply of food, extra clothing, cooking kit, and sleeping bags neatly stored inside. They'd made it through the first night unmolested.

Bill and his small group could see their tent from where the Beaver was tied down. The camp was empty, but the photographers should have stayed at home—they'd have gotten some dandy bear pictures right at their own campsite.

Walleye shuffled down a nearby bear trail and crossed to the other side of the creek. He must have smelled something from the tent; instead of passing it by, he stopped and tore a gaping hole in the side of the thin nylon. It collapsed like a parachute hitting the ground; within moments, Bill could see down feathers from a sleeping bag drifting away on the gentle breeze. Slashing the pile of belongings with three-inch-long claws on both front feet, Walleye located the fresh food and ate it.

Moments later, the bear found the cardboard box containing their canned food, beer, and soft drinks. Each container popped, squirted, or dripped as Walleye bit into it, including the dozen fresh eggs which dribbled from his chin.

John and Ben went back upstream fishing again, but Bill waited on the beach for another three hours for the photographers to return. When they finally had to leave, Bill circled the area and spotted the Norwegians two miles upstream photographing a sow with two little cubs. There was nothing Bill and John could do for them now; the photographers were on their own until morning.

Bill, John, and Ben returned to Dream Creek early the next day. When they arrived, the two Norwegians were standing on the beach. Their camp was gone; two back packs and a duffel bag were lying on the sand beside them.

Both men spoke English. Lars, the taller of the pair, with long blond hair and sparkling blue eyes, explained what had happened. The bear had returned while they were trying to find something to eat. Neither of them carried any weapons or even a fishing rod, and quickly retreated to the beach. When the bear left the camp an hour later they returned, cleaned up the mess, and carried everything back to the lake. They'd been on the beach all night.

Bill asked Lars if they needed a ride back to Iliamna. They thanked him but declined, explaining that their own pilot was supposed to pick them up later in the morning.

"But if you have any food to spare," he said, and left the sentence hanging. John broke open his pack and gave them each a sandwich, some cookies, and an apple before they left to go fishing.

Cal circled overhead, then landed in the lake an hour later. He picked up the campers and left, only to return an hour later, and Bill guessed he was bringing more campers. Forty-five minutes after his second departure, Cal was back with another load, confirming Bill's suspicions. At 4:00 p.m., Ben finally had enough fishing for the day and they started back down the creek toward the Beaver, Bill in the lead and John bringing up the rear.

They were walking along the right bank of the creek and had just turned the last bend heading downstream. Three hundred yards from the lake Bill spotted something in the brush a hundred feet ahead. At first, he thought the big, brown mass was the underground root-structure of a fallen tree, but then it twitched slightly. Bill stopped abruptly. "Come up here, John," he called.

Ben stepped off the bear trail and allowed John to pass. "What is it, boss?"

The only other time Bill had seen a bear hide along a trail was on Kodiak Island 15 years ago. That time, the bear was preparing to charge. "Load," Bill ordered, and jacked a round into the chamber of his rifle. John did the same. They'd both started carrying a weapon again, knowing Walleye was still around.

"Ho, bear," Bill called. The bear moved again, creeping closer to the trail. "Ho, bear! What's going on!" he shouted more loudly.

Walleye stood up, less than a hundred feet away. His brown head swayed back and forth over the brushline as he stared at them. Ten seconds later he dropped back on all four feet and strolled toward the creek, crossing the trail they were walking on.

"What was that all about, Bill?" Ben asked.

"I wish I knew." Still watching the bear, they started walking slowly toward the lake.

Walleye stopped on the gravel bar just inside the river mouth on their side of the creek. There were thousands of salmon holding in the deep water in front of him, waiting their turn to move upriver to spawn. They covered the bottom of the creek, stretching bank to bank and several fish deep. The pool looked like a crowded fish bowl and the closest fish was only ten feet in front of the bear.

Walleye charged into the water, causing a small tidal wave across the pool. A thousand salmon streaked downstream toward the lake, driving a foot-high wall of water in front of them. Walleye continued swimming across the creek and climbed up on the opposite bank.

"Uh-oh," John said, pointing across the river. "There's going to be trouble. Walleye's heading for the new campers."

"Shouldn't you warn them?" Ben asked.

"We couldn't get there in time to do much good, anyway," Bill said. "There's no way to keep that bear from tearing apart any camp he finds—except to shoot it—and I don't want to shoot it." They stayed put and watched.

Bill could see four men; two were already fishing at the stream mouth, where the salmon were stacked up by the hundreds, and two were still at the camp.

Their camp consisted of one large, blue tent with an attached awning. It covered their cooking and eating area; three smaller, khaki-colored tents on the perimeter of the site were for sleeping. Walleye headed directly toward the largest tent.

"Hey, you guys!" John shouted. "Bear coming!"

"What?" A man with a white apron called back. He was almost two hundred yards away and could hardly hear them.

"Bear! Bear!" Bill, John, and Ben shouted together. As the man rushed around the tent to see what they were shouting about, Walleye tore a six-foot-long hole in the blue tarp. The grizzly marched into their kitchen.

The two men screamed at the bear, cursing and yelling at the top of their voices. Walleye looked at them for a moment, then buried his head in a box and pulled out a piece of meat.

"Get out of here, you no good sonofabitch!" the man in the apron shouted. He advanced into the mouth of the tent and struck the bear on the head with a broom. Give him credit for a lot of guts, but not much common sense!

The bear huffed and charged out of the tent at the cook; the man fled in terror down toward the lake. Walleye took a few more steps toward the man, saw him stumble and almost fall before catching himself. Only after the cook and his companion reached the beach did the grizzly turn back to the box of steaks. He ate all six, then dug around looking for more food. Twenty minutes later he wandered away toward the beach himself, stopped a few hundred yards away from the campers, and lay down on the sand.

Bill crossed the stream. Cal wasn't around and Bill could tell that these new guys needed some advice. Ben and John followed.

When they approached, the man in the apron spoke up in a broad Texas drawl. "Did you see what that SOB did?" he said, rummaging through the devastation inside the large tent. "What kind of bears you got around here, anyway?"

"Grizzlies," Bill said.

"Are they all that mean?" he asked, lifting his fancy cowboy hat to scratch his head. He introduced himself as Clarence Pitts, a short, wiry man with gray hair at the temples.

"Some of them," Bill said. "Didn't Cal say anything about the bears before he brought you over here?"

"Hell, no. Cal didn't say anything about bears."

Bill asked him if he could look around, and Clarence showed him where the bear had been. Bill picked up a large, empty plastic bag marked 'Potatoes, Dried,' and asked if it had been full when they arrived.

"That was supposed to be a week's supply of fried potatoes," Clarence said. "We were going to live on fish, fried potatoes, and beer." They were lucky Walleye didn't find the beer.

Bill already knew Walleye liked fish and beer; now he knew the bear liked dried potatoes, too. Looking over the man's shoulder, Bill could see the boar belly-deep in the lake drinking water. The dried potatoes had probably absorbed all the fluids in his stomach; he looked bloated as a hog when he walked back to the beach and flopped down on the sand again.

"You think he'll be back?" Clarence asked.

"Count on it," John said. "As soon as he digests what he ate, he'll be back for more. He knows the food's here."

"How in hell does he know that?"

They let that question pass. "Are you going to stay here tonight?" Bill asked.

"We were going to stay for a week," one of the other Texans said, moving in to join the conversation. He was taller than Clarence, with red hair and a full mustache. "Cal's due back here in an hour with the rest of the camp and two more guys."

"What makes you so sure the bear will be back?" Clarence asked again.

"That same bear raised hell with the Swedes Cal brought here last week, and the Norwegians that he brought here two days ago," Bill said, "and they didn't have half the food you guys have." From the quizzical look on the cook's face, Bill knew that Cal hadn't told them about the photographers either. Bill nodded toward the lake. "He'll be back."

"How soon?" Ben asked.

"Maybe an hour, maybe six hours," John said, turning to look at the doctor. "Why?"

"I'd like to stay and watch," he said. "Maybe have some coffee, take some more pictures." John hadn't noticed Ben filming the whole thing with his pocket camera.

Bill looked at John; they both shrugged and nodded, then left and crossed back to their own side of the creek. A fresh pot of hobo coffee sounded pretty good to Bill, too.

Walleye stood up on the beach an hour later just as Cal circled overhead. The bear started toward the campsite while Cal landed. The bear got there first.

All four campers were armed with pots and pans. When Walleye was still a hundred feet away, each of them started shouting and beating on the pots with sticks.

The commotion caused the bear to stop and stand up, his small ears cocked forward. Half-a-minute later, he dropped back on all four feet and started toward the camp again. Cal was still far out in the lake taxiing toward the shore.

The Texans doubled their efforts to drive the bear

away, shouting, cursing, and pounding on the pots and pans as hard as they could, but Walleye couldn't be turned back. When the bear reached the blue tent, the cook drew a pistol from a holster hidden under his coat and aimed the gun at Walleye's face only thirty feet away from him.

Pop! Pop! The light pistol lacked the explosive crack of a high-powered rifle or shotgun.

When Clarence fired, Walleye wheeled on his hind feet and ran back into the alders. Furious at this new turn of events, Bill ran back over to the camp.

"What the hell do you think you're doing, Clarence?" he said, grabbing the pistol away from him. "This is no weapon to use on a bear." Over the cook's shoulder he saw Cal's airplane nudge onto the beach.

"It's only bird shot," Clarence said. "I wasn't trying to kill it; just scare it away."

"You scared him all right," Bill said, "but if you hit him in the eyes, you've also blinded him, or partially blinded him, which is even worse. Did you think of that?" Bill ejected the remaining shells onto the ground and handed the .38 Special revolver back to the cook.

"Serves the sonofabitch right," Clarence said as Cal came panting up the beach toward them. He was waving his shotgun in front of him.

"What the hell are you doing on this side of the river?" Cal shouted in Bill's face, not yet bothering to ask about the camp, or the bear, or his clients. His face turned crimson as he raged at Bill. "Get back on your side of the river or I'll blow your ass to hell and back."

"These guys just tried to help us," Clarence said.

"Help, hell," Cal said. "If they wanted to help they'd shoot that goddamn bear and be done with it." He turned back to look at Bill, jacking a round into the chamber of his shotgun.

"Get the hell away from me, Bascomb," Cal said, scowling and furious, his eyes boring into his enemy. "Get away from me if you know what's good for you."

If Bill and John hadn't had their own rifles with them, they agreed later that Cal would have shot Bill on the spot.

"That bear will be back, Clarence," Bill said, turning to leave. "And if you wounded it, he's going to be madder than hell."

23

Janet made the granola herself, adding plenty of nuts and raisins and other dried fruits to the 7-grain cereal she ordered from the health food store in Anchorage. Bill ate some every morning; today he'd have enjoyed it more if he hadn't tossed and turned all night worrying about what Walleye was going to do next. The bear had become too unpredictable, his personality and character had changed for the worse, and it wasn't safe for the average human to be on the same river with him. Overnight stays at Dream Creek could now be frightfully dangerous.

The overcast, gray day outside the dining room windows did little to ease his mind. The blue skies, warm temperatures, and light winds they'd been having for the past three weeks were over; he didn't have to call the weather bureau to know a storm was coming.

"Somebody's got to do something about Walleye, Charlie," Bill said, pushing his bowl away and reaching for his third cup of coffee. It wasn't up to Bill to tell Charlie how to run his business, but he felt that he had to make a few comments. His churning stomach demanded it, if nothing else.

Charlie had also had a sleepless night. "I already called Jim Roberts," he said. "His wife told me that Jim was still in King Salmon. She didn't expect to see him all week."

"Jim or not, we shouldn't take any more fishermen to Dream Creek," Bill stated firmly. "At least until Walleye either leaves or cools down and starts acting like a friendly bear again."

"What's going to change him?" Janet asked, joining them at the table. This was the same conversation they'd had last night; she knew as much as the rest of them.

Bill shrugged and looked at Charlie; he shrugged back. Nobody was going to change that bear now, and they both knew it. The only thing they could do was warn the other operators who fished on Dream Creek. Charlie started with Iliamna Skytaxi, then the other lodges in the area. Finally he called Cal.

"You're using that goddamn speaker phone again, aren't you?" Cal said—no hello, no good morning, nothing. "Well, if that goddamn brother-in-law of yours is listening, I'm telling him right now to keep the hell away from my guests. Scared the hell out of them, that's what he's done, and I won't have it, you hear me, Bascomb?" There was a two second pause while Cal caught his breath. "Now, what do you want, Charlie?"

Charlie started to describe what had happened between Walleye and the Texans. "Hell, I know all that," Cal interrupted. "Clarence told me all about it; said he chased that bear away with a pistol, and if Bascomb hadn't butted in and scared the hell out of the other guys, they'd be fishing on Dream Creek right now."

Charlie gave Bill a thumbs-up sign, and smiled. Cal had moved the campers back last night, just as they thought he would. That's what all the airplane activity after dinner had been about.

Turning back to the phone, Charlie asked, "Are you going back there?"

"Most of the Texans chickened out. They're camping on the Newhalen now," Cal said. "Clarence and I are going to Dream Creek this morning. What's it to you, anyway?"

"I've been here over 20 years, Cal, and I've never seen a bear act that way before," Charlie said. "He was stalking our group yesterday before he tore your camp apart. I'd leave it alone for a while. At least don't camp over there."

"You don't say," Cal said, sarcastically. "Well, that son-of-a-bitch doesn't scare me, and I'm not through with him yet. If the Park Service can run the bears off the Brooks River with cracker shells and rubber bullets, I guess I can do the same on Dream Creek."

Charlie tried one last appeal. "There're plenty of other places to fish around here," he said. "You don't have to take chances on Dream Creek."

"I've told you before and I'm telling you now!" Cal shouted into the phone. He had the patience of a lit firecracker. "Mind your own goddamn business and stay out of my way!" The line went dead.

Bill poured Charlie another cup of coffee and waited for him to cool off. "What's all that talk about cracker shells and rubber bullets?" he asked.

"The new superintendent at Katmai thinks they can control the bears by shooting at them with special shotgun loads," Charlie said.

"Rubber bullets I understand, but what's a cracker shell?"

"It's a special kind of fire cracker that they load in a

shotgun. They fire it at a bear and, when it goes off under his feet, it's supposed to scare him away."

"That's about the dumbest thing I've ever heard," Bill said. "What if they miss the bear and the fire cracker goes off on the other side of him. That could scare the bear right back toward the shooter!"

John walked into the dining room and sat down to breakfast, catching the last part of Bill's comment. "What are you talking about now?" he asked. Charlie explained the cracker shell idea.

"What do you think, Dad?"

"They claim it works sometimes, but I'm not so sure," Charlie answered. "There're too many variables: different bears, inexperienced shooters, varying field conditions. Bill pointed out only the most obvious problem but there's got to be a lot more potentially explosive situations that nobody has even thought of yet. I've heard that some rangers are even using a little bird shot on the bears when they feel the need."

"Lead would sting a little more than rubber bullets, but I don't like any of it," Bill said, shaking his head.

"I don't either," Charlie agreed. "There's always that one bear that won't respond to anything the way it's expected to. Shoot at him too much and, eventually, he's going to react the wrong way and hurt somebody. That's my opinion, anyway."

"The Brooks River is in a National Park, isn't it?" Janet said, more as a statement than a question. She'd been listening quietly, first to Cal on the phone, then her husband and brother, and getting madder and madder. Her face was set in a frown, her eyes pinched, her nose quivering. "They shouldn't be firing guns in a National Park, anyway!"

"I guess if they run it, they can do anything they want to," Charlie said, and shrugged again.

Janet threw her hands up in despair, upsetting her cup,

spilling steaming coffee on the linen cloth. "Isn't there any place left where the bears can live and not get shot at?" she said. "These bears need space, not crowding and hostility every time they see a human."

"Hey, honey," Charlie said, getting out of his seat to walk over to his wife's chair. He put his hand on her shoulder. "Bill and John aren't pushing that bear. They're trying to stay out of its way."

"I know that," she said, calmer. She covered Charlie's hand with her own. "It's just that Park Service stuff that set me off. Where's it all going to end—like Yellowstone where they had to kill all those bears because they were trained to eat garbage?"

None of them answered her—none of them could. Maybe she was right.

After they'd sopped up the coffee, John asked the same question that was on Bill's mind. "Do you really think Cal is going to use rubber bullets?"

"Not for a second, John," Charlie said. He hoisted his bulky frame out of his chair and stalked out of the room. When they heard the front door slam a few seconds later, they knew Charlie was headed for the hangar.

Bill probably should have let it go, too, but he couldn't get Walleye out of his mind. Ben finally got tired of watching him pace back and forth, went out to find Charlie, and asked if Bill could take him back to Dream Creek. The trout fishing had been really good despite the bear problems. Charlie agreed, but for the first time all summer, he reminded Bill to take his rifle.

"How long are you going to stay there?" Janet asked.

"Just a few hours," Ben said. "I have to take the evening flight back to town; they need me in the hospital tomorrow."

"Then I'm going with you," she said. "John, you might as well tag along. I'll get Mel to pack a lunch and we'll have a picnic on the beach."

"In the rain?" Bill could see spatters on the windows.

"If we must," Janet said. She wasn't smiling when she stood up and headed for the kitchen—end of discussion. They took off shortly before noon.

Cal's airplane was moored to the beach next to the campsite; the large, blue tent and another smaller one were set up the same place they'd used yesterday. Bill circled over the river and saw Cal and Clarence half-a-mile upstream standing on the downstream side of a long gravel bar. Salmon were spawning almost at their feet. Walleye had walked to within a hundred feet upstream of them before they spotted him.

As soon as Clarence saw the bear, he started running downstream through the ripples; soon Cal was matching him stride for stride. Bill circled again, a thousand feet in the air over the creek.

Walleye watched the pair for a second or two, paying no attention to the aircraft circling overhead. Then he started loping downstream, quickly gaining ground on the two fishermen who were struggling through calf-deep water in their hip boots. Cal turned to look at the bear and stumbled as one of his feet fell into a freshly-dug salmon redd. Catching his balance again, he loped after Clarence, with the bear just fifty feet from his heels. Walleye was just loafing along through the shallows. He could have caught either man in seconds if he'd wanted to.

Cal had already lost his fishing rod; now he shrugged out of his pack and dropped it in the shallow water. The bear stopped to tear the pack apart as the two fishermen ran around the next bend. They returned to their camp while Bill landed and taxied to the beach.

"You stay the hell out of here, Bascomb," Cal shouted across the creek as they climbed out of the Beaver. He had his shotgun in his hands and Bill didn't doubt that he'd use it—on him or the bears. Bill turned his back and didn't bother to answer.

"Can we fish a little, Bill?" Ben asked.

"Yeah, sure, but just here at the mouth," he said. "Don't walk upstream. I want everybody to stay close to the airplane."

Fifteen minutes later John lit a fire and heated some water. They were gathered around the coals, sipping hot tea and eating some cookies from the lunchbox when Walleye appeared on the beach.

"Get out of here, Mr. Bear!" Bill shouted, a rifle cradled in his arm.

Walleye stopped a hundred feet away and stood looking at them. He turned sideways, then faced them again and stood up, his enormous head towering ten feet above the sand. The bear was well over 700 pounds now. His heavy, chocolate-brown hide was still half-wet from fishing all morning; it clung to his powerful frame, outlining the thick neck, muscular shoulders, front and hind legs. Small, charcoal eyes stared right at Bill.

"Get out of here!" Bill shouted again and lobbed a small branch at the bear.

Walleye dropped back to all four feet and continued walking toward them slowly. "Everybody, back into the Beaver," Bill ordered, grabbing the lunchbox. He shoved it at John.

When the bear was fifty feet away, Bill climbed into the plane himself and started the engine. They weren't going anywhere; the two mooring lines were still tied to the trees. As soon as the oil-pressure gauge steadied at 60 pounds, he revved up the still-warm engine to half-throttle.

As soon as the engine started, Walleye stopped walking and stood up again. When the engine roared, the bear turned away and ran back into the brush. Five minutes later after Bill had shut down the engine and they had returned to the beach, Bill saw Walleye cross the creek and head toward Cal's camp.

Walleye walked up to the rear of the big, blue tent.

When he ripped a five-foot tear in it, Cal and Clarence came stumbling out the door, cursing and shouting. Walleye backed up ten feet, then jumped toward them and tore another big slash in the tent.

Clarence drew his pistol. As Walleye stepped over the packs laying along the back of the tent and started toward the food, Clarence fired. This time Walleye didn't run away—he charged at Clarence, knocked him down, and bit into his arm.

Clarence screamed in pain and tried to fend off the bear with his other arm. Unaffected, Walleye picked the man up by the shoulder and shook him like a rag doll. When Clarence went limp, Cal aimed his shotgun at the bear.

Blam! Blam! Before the shots from both barrels had echoed across the hills and down the lake, the bear had dropped Clarence and charged toward Cal, who was fumbling to jam two more shells into his gun. The bear was on top of him before he could reload.

At the first shot, Bill grabbed his own rifle and ran toward their camp. Crossing the creek slowed him down and put their camp out of view; it took a minute before he could see what was happening—but he could hear it. Blood-curdling growls and snarls from the bear were mixed with Cal's screams for help. After Bill cleared the creek, he climbed the bank and ran toward the camp.

First he saw Walleye, then Cal's head and shoulders underneath the bear. Cal had stopped screaming but the bear was still chewing on his head and upper torso. Shouldering his rifle, Bill aimed at Walleye's left front shoulder.

Crack! The 300-grain slug hit the large shoulder bone and knocked Walleye down on top of Cal.

Instantly, the wounded grizzly jumped back to his feet. Before Bill could reload for a second shot, the bear ran around the tent on three legs and back toward the alders. Leaping over Cal's prostrate form, Bill chased after Walleye for a second shot but lost track of him as he fled through the small trees. He fired twice more at the moving shadow anyway—grizzlies are seldom killed with one shot. Bill knew that; he also knew that he'd eventually have to finish what he'd started.

John ran up to join his uncle. Bill handed him the rifle and told him to stand watch in case the bear returned. "Ben, get over here—fast!" he shouted, running back to the two injured men.

Cal had suffered the worst, but he was still breathing. When Bill rolled him over on his back to check for a pulse, he saw again what the savage fury of an enraged bear could do. It was a blessing that Cal was unconscious.

He'd been scalped, with patches of hair and skin hanging from his head—why do the bears always seem to go for the head? His left ear was shredded; the left side of his face bore tooth and claw marks that exposed the jagged edges of cheek and jaw bones. Fresh, bright blood surged through holes in his shirt by his left shoulder, and his left arm jutted from the bloody torso at an unusual angle.

"Get the first aid kit," Ben said, rushing up to take over the examination. He started ripping away Cal's clothing while Bill took off at a run for the plane. A few minutes later, Bill returned with Janet, the first aid kit, and spare blankets.

Ben was ripping his own shirt into strips. "Check Clarence, Bill," Ben said. "Janet, you stay here, I'll need help with Cal."

Clarence had managed to pull himself up to a sitting position. "I think my arm is broken," he said, as Bill crouched beside him. His face was pale and his breathing was very shallow. Bill took off his jacket, put it over the cook's shoulders, and laid him back down again, raising his feet to rest on one of the packs.

"Just lie here a minute," Bill said. "The doctor will be over to look at you as soon as he takes care of Cal."

"I need your knife, Bill," Ben shouted. He was having

trouble trying to tear Cal's clothing away from his wounds. Bill sprinted back to help.

"No, you keep it," Ben said, when Bill tried to hand him the knife. "Cut here," he stretched the fabric, "and here. Janet, hold here, good, cut here, now there." Ben's fingers were flying as Bill and Janet responded to his orders. When they finally exposed the shoulder, the wound looked ghastly. Two bones were sticking out of the skin, and blood was spurting from a deep cut near his neck. Ben covered the bleeding with several gauze pads and told Janet to press them tightly against his body.

"For God's sake, don't let go!"

24

"I can't do any more for him here," Ben said. He'd almost stopped the flow of blood; only a small amount now oozed out from under the gauze between Janet's fingers. "If you can get him to the hospital in Anchorage, he has a chance. Otherwise?" Ben looked up at Bill; his eyes said the rest.

"John," Bill called. He was still watching for the bear, but it was time to get out of there. John appeared from around the tent, looking over his shoulder.

"Leave the rifle here and go down and take all the seats out of the Beaver, except mine and the copilot's. Then come back." John ran toward the lake as Bill picked up the gun—Walleye was still out there—somewhere.

John was back in five minutes.

"We'll use the blanket for a stretcher," Ben said. He'd quickly taken charge of the medical emergency, smoothly directing the others to do his bidding. "Bill, you take one side, John and I will take the other. Janet, walk alongside and don't let the pressure off that gauze pad for a second. We'll do the rest."

Clarence started to get to his feet as they passed him with the makeshift stretcher.

"Don't get up," Ben said. "We'll be right back." Clarence sank back to the ground, a grimace of pain showing with every movement.

They loaded Cal and Clarence into the Beaver and Bill flew everyone to Iliamna, making radio contact with the Iliamna Flight Service Station as soon as he'd gained enough altitude to clear the hills. A medivac jet was airborne from Anchorage to Iliamna before they landed.

Cal was still unconscious, but alive, when they loaded him and Clarence aboard the jet. Ben went too, to direct and help the Emergency Medical Technician assigned to the flight, then to the hospital to help the surgeon on duty in the emergency ward.

When Bill and John got back to the lodge, Bill went straight to his room and picked up more ammunition. Janet was in the lounge, and called to him as he walked through. She knew what was on his mind. "Are you going back there?" she asked.

"I have to," Bill said, "and I want to take John with me."

"You've already risked your life once today for that idiot," she said, pointing across the bay at Cal's lodge. "It'll be dark soon; why push it?"

"I have to, sis," Bill said, shrugging into his flying jacket. "Sure, he's an idiot—more than that, he's a spoiled brat who's never really grown up—and I've known that ever since I met him. But I'm still partly responsible for starting this whole thing and I'm going to finish the job."

Janet took a deep breath and exhaled slowly. She looked down toward the bay where the Beaver was parked, then back at her brother. Deep lines furrowed her brow, a whitish pallor colored the skin stretched tightly over each cheekbone.

"You're determined to do this thing, aren't you?" she asked quietly.

"Yes."

"Then he'd better take John," Charlie said. He'd been listening from the corner; now he crossed over and put an arm around his wife. "Honey, you know I'd go if I could."

"I know that," she said. "But I wouldn't be any happier, and you don't have to tell me that two guns are better than one."

"That's right," Charlie said.

Janet took one more sigh, then straightened her back and turned to her brother. "Then what are you waiting for? Get to it." It was an order.

John grabbed his rifle and jacket, and they left immediately. At 7:30 p.m. they were back in the air again; by 8:00, the Beaver was tied down on the beach alongside Cal's plane. They had an hour of daylight left, then an hour of dusk, then pitch black. There'd be no moon that night.

The rain was heavier at Dream Creek, pushed along by a 20-knot wind. Bill knew it would get worse as the front approached; more rain, more wind, maybe fog. Visibility down the lake was down to three miles, inside the alders it would be much less. He picked up his rifle, loaded the magazine, and put one round in the chamber. John did the same, then followed Bill to the edge of the alders where he'd last seen the bear.

"I hit him in the left shoulder and knocked him down," Bill said, reviewing what he knew for John one more time. "Walleye jumped right back up and ran away on three legs, dragging his left foot. I fired twice more, but he was already in the alders and I don't think I hit him again. If you get a shot, aim for the right front shoulder. If we can break both front legs, we've got him."

"Did Cal hit the bear when he shot at it?"

"I don't know. He was using 00-Buck in his shotgun—probably meant for me—I checked the empty shell casings. The last time I saw a bear hit with buck shot, the pellets barely penetrated through the skin. We've got to assume he was only hit once."

"How about the other guy?" John wanted to know as much as he could, and Bill patiently explained. John was taking a chance, too.

"All Clarence had was the same pistol you saw yesterday," Bill said. "He could have gotten lucky and hit him in the eyes with bird shot but I don't think so. A blinded bear would have knocked some trees down when he ran away through the alders. I'm assuming the only thing wrong with Walleye is a broken and very painful left shoulder."

"He's also mad as hell," John said.

"He is that," Bill agreed, "and he can run almost as fast on three legs as he can on four. Any more questions?"

"Nope." The way John said it told Bill he was ready.

There was a chance that Walleye was already dead. It had been two hours since the shooting; if Bill's bullet had ricocheted off the shoulder and hit a vital organ, the bear would have bled to death by now. Bill's tactics for the stalk did not count on it.

"John, when we get into the alders, I want you to concentrate on the blood trail. You've always been a good tracker, but some of the blood may have already been washed away in the rain. Keep that in mind. I'll walk right behind you watching for the bear."

"Okay."

"There's no need to keep quiet—if he's alive, Walleye will hear us."

"Okay."

"And one more thing," and Bill looked at him closely.

"If he comes at us, it'll be sudden—no warning—and you may only get a quick shot. Take what you can get; if you see any hair in your sights, pull the trigger. Even if you can't see the sights, pull the trigger anyway. One of us has to get him before he gets us."

Once they entered the alders, their forward and lateral visibility was reduced to less than 50 feet. John crept slowly forward, bent over at the waist, his eyes on the ground; Bill was five feet behind him. There wasn't a lot of blood, but the few drops every foot or two was enough to follow the track.

"Hold it," Bill said, a few moments after they'd entered the brush. He pointed to the trunk of an eight-inch-thick alder to the right of the trail. The side facing the clearing had a half-inch ragged hole three feet off the ground, the opposite side had been blown away, and jagged splinters of white wood edged the hole. "Here's where one of my bullets went."

John nodded and they started forward again. The bear had run straight through the first thick patch of alders, across an open field where they almost lost the track because of the rain, and then into the next alder patch. A hundred feet into the second stand of trees John stopped. "I lost it," he said.

"Where was the last drop?" Bill asked.

"About three feet back."

Bill backed up five feet, with his eyes still rapidly scanning the surrounding brush. John retraced his own steps and located the last drop he'd seen.

"Make a small circle, John," Bill said. "Maybe he's changed course."

"Here it is," John said, a minute later. The bear had turned left toward a small hill and they started forward again, climbing slowly.

"Hold it," John said quietly. "He's changed course again." John was peering toward the right now, spotted another drop and stepped past it. When he found the next drop, he turned back to look at Bill. "I think he's circling, boss."

Bill looked at his watch—9:30 already—it was getting darker. The low hummocks of earth and shrubs that he could see all looked like a bear crouched down and waiting. He motioned for John to continue. If they didn't find the bear in the next 15 minutes he'd have to call the search off until full daylight in the morning. By that time, the rain would have washed all the blood away and they might never find him.

Ten minutes later they were walking in a straight line again. The bear had made a small circle and then continued on in the same direction he'd been running. John found some blood three feet off the ground on the trunk of an alder, then some more on another tree. He pointed them out. "He's bleeding from the shoulder wound."

Two minutes later John stopped again. "Lost it," he said.

They were on the side of a small knoll with alders and willows all around them. Bill couldn't see more than 30 feet in any direction. "Back up, John."

"I got it now," John said, pointing up the hill. He started moving again and Bill grabbed hold of his jacket.

"He's close," Bill said. "I can feel it." The hillside, the thick brush, the semidarkness all crowded his senses. Stooping, he picked up a dead branch and threw it as far as he could up the hill. It clattered loudly against a tree and fell to the ground.

A branch snapped to the right of where Bill had thrown the stick. Both hunters turned instinctively—the bear was charging at them through the trees. On the wet leaves, Walleye wasn't making a sound; if he hadn't broken that twig, in the fading light they might not have seen him.

By the time they raised their rifles the bear was only 20 feet away. Both guns fired at the same time. With a blood-curdling roar, the bear crashed headlong to the earth between them.

Bill quickly reloaded and fired another shot at the bear's neck. The ear-splitting snarls finally faded into gurgles. Walleye died at his feet.

Bill was shaking like a leaf in a hurricane, sweat oozing out of every pore on his body. He and John fell to the ground with Walleye between them, the bear's vacant eyes staring straight ahead, his lips still curled back in a defiant snarl.

Bill didn't say a word, just sat there with a lump as big as an apple in his throat.

Five minutes later, John asked, "You all right, boss?"

"Yeah, John, I'm all right," Bill said, leaning back against a tree, not trusting his legs to support him yet. "How about yourself?"

"Shaky."

"Let's sit here a few more minutes," Bill said.

They could hear the wind whistling through the higher branches of the alders surrounding them, but it was relatively quiet under the canopy of trees. Each man sat with his own thoughts, neither of them looking at the dead bear. Bill finally broke the silence.

"I can tell you one thing for certain, John," he said, slowly and somberly. "This is the last bear I'll ever kill."

25

Epilogue

I didn't hear about the death of Walleye until Bill came back to Kodiak that fall. He told me what happened in his matter-of-fact way, then surprised the devil out of me when he also said that he'd given his hunting camp to his nephew, John.

"I used to think I knew a lot about grizzlies," Bill said, "but I really didn't know anything compared to Charlie. He's the guy who knows; he's the guy who has to work around them all summer, keep his fishermen and other guests out of trouble and still try to make a living."

I gently reminded Bill that he'd been rather successful himself as a hunting guide for the past 20-plus years, and that most of the world now thought of him as an expert on grizzlies. He had an answer to that, too.

"Before I started to help Janet and Charlie, all I really knew about the bears was how to stalk them and kill them and skin them. Sure, I knew the kind of terrain they like and the food they like and where they hibernate, but I always treated them as a class, just a species to be hunted for the pleasure of man.

"Charlie, on the other hand, treats each bear as an individual, with a personality all its own. Take old Blondie for instance, the sow that never let her cubs get close to humans. Charlie and John knew that, they'd watched her for years. They'd also watched The Warden, incidentally, one of the smartest and craftiest bears I've ever seen; even Miss Paine, who'd march her cubs to within a hundred feet of us—and then watch us and them like a hawk. Charlie has to deal with these bears all the time, and to do that, he's got to really know about bears. The last thing that Charlie thinks about is having to shoot a grizzly. There are just too many other things to consider first."

"Then what happened with Walleye?" I asked.

"This is what Charlie thinks," Bill said. "He thinks it started when he was still a cub, and somebody like Ike or Randy or Cal started feeding salmon to his mother. When he was three years old and his mother kicked him out of the nest, so to speak, Walleye continued doing exactly what his mother had taught him—he started bothering people for salmon. Charlie and John saw it happen but couldn't do much about it. The more Walleye got fed, the more he begged, and the more he begged, the more he got fed. The conditioning feeds on itself, no pun intended, and the bear eventually lost his natural fear of humans. When that happened, his fate was sealed. If Cal hadn't shot him, somebody else would have had to.

"Walleye didn't need to die—that's the part that troubles all of us. He'd been programmed to survive. He was large for his age, he was aggressive, he was fat and healthy, he should have lived another 20 years and sired dozens of cubs just like him. Now he's history."

Then I asked, "Does Charlie have any ideas why The Warden, or Miss Paine, or most of the other bears didn't fall into the same trap?"

"'They're all individuals,' Charlie liked to say. 'Some are smarter. Maybe some are luckier.'"

• • •

Bill also told me that Cal survived the mauling. He lost one eye, and the skin that finally grew back on his scalp was discolored and scarred. His shoulder was broken in three places, and his left arm was damaged so severely they had to amputate halfway between his shoulder and elbow. He spent two months in the hospital, then went through several more months of physical therapy. Before it was all over, Cal had sold his lodge to another outsider, someone from California, Charlie thinks, and said he'd never return to Alaska.

Alaska won't miss Cal, either—but the state still has no regulations in effect establishing acceptable qualifications for owning or operating either a fishing lodge or outfitting company that chooses to shepherd humans in and out of the bush.

• • •

That next spring, Bill promised me a special present for my 70th birthday. Four hours before the lowest tide of May, he flew me to the same clam beach on the shores of Kamishak Bay where he'd taken the photographers two years ago. The air temperature was in the 50's, the sky a brilliant blue, the wind a gentle five knots from the west. From Anchorage to Adak, all the coastal weather stations were reporting ideal flying conditions.

We arrived on the clam beach at 9:45 a.m., an hour before low tide. Charlie, Janet, and John met us 15 minutes later; that was the part of the surprise that Bill hadn't told me about. John had his private pilot's license now, and had brought his family in Charlie's Beaver.

We'd been there half-an-hour, enjoying the sunshine, digging a few clams, sipping coffee, and reminiscing about old times, when a sow grizzly with three cubs walked onto the beach a quarter mile away and started to dig her own clams. The small cubs weighed no more than twenty pounds apiece, and followed their mother's every step, stopping when she stopped, moving when she moved. The two smaller cubs were tan-colored, the larger a dark chocolate, with a small white band on one side of its neck.

"Do you think Walleye could be the father?" Janet asked, looking at the trio of cubs through her small set of binoculars.

"Could be either Walleye or The Warden, or some other boar, for that matter," Charlie answered, letting his own glasses fall back on the lanyard around his neck. "But it really doesn't matter who its father is. If we humans don't clean up our act out here, there'll be more hell to pay on Dream Creek six years from now."

As usual, Charlie was right about that, too.